Why did the sight of Daniel Brantley still cause her knees to sway, even when he'd upset her?

She took a deep breath and told him exactly what was on her mind. "I'm not going anywhere, Daniel. I'm staying right here in Claremont with our nephew."

"Me, too."

"Then we need to come up with how this is going to work, because I promised my sister I'd take care of Kaden, and I'm not about to break that promise. I love Kaden."

"I know." He pulled out a chair from the table and sat down as though he totally belonged here in the middle of her home and in the middle of her life. Suddenly Mandy realized that if he was determined to help raise Kaden, too, then that's where he'd be, in the middle of her life from now on.

Mandy and Daniel, working together to raise a child, forever.

Books by Renee Andrews

Love Inspired

Her Valentine Family
Healing Autumn's Heart
Picture Perfect Family

RENEE ANDREWS

spends a lot of time in the gym. No, she isn't working out. Her husband, a former All-American gymnast, co-owns ACE Cheer Company, an all-star cheerleading company. She is thankful the talented kids at the gym don't have a problem when she brings her laptop and writes while they sweat. When she isn't writing, she's typically traveling with her husband, bragging about their two sons or spoiling their bulldog.

Renee is a kidney donor and actively supports organ donation. She welcomes prayer requests and loves to hear from readers! Write to her at Renee@ReneeAndrews.com, visit her website at www.reneeandrews.com or check her out on Facebook or Twitter.

Picture Perfect Family
Renee Andrews

Love Inspired

Recycling programs for this product may not exist in your area.

 ™ LOVE INSPIRED BOOKS

ISBN-13: 978-0-373-81611-8

PICTURE PERFECT FAMILY

www.LoveInspiredBooks.com

Printed in U.S.A.

Whoever welcomes a little child like this
in my name welcomes me.
—*Matthew* 18:5

This novel is dedicated to Gina Bowers Brown,
my amazing and beautiful sister.

"A sister is a little bit of childhood
that can never be lost."
—Marion C. Garretty

Chapter One

"So I guess Kaden's excited that Daniel Brantley is back in town, huh?"

Mandy Carter couldn't control the natural flinch that Jessica Martin's question provoked. Consequently, the perfect photograph she'd been about to take turned into a distorted mess when her normally steady hand jerked the camera. Instead of capturing Nathan and Lainey Martin giggling atop two bales of hay by the pond at Hydrangea Park, she got a blurred picture of the grass around her feet.

"Wait, hold on, let's try that again," she coaxed the kids, but the two-year-old had turned her attention from her brother to the buckles at the top of her pink overalls, and a group of bicyclists passing by had piqued Nathan's interest.

"Oh, sorry," Jessica apologized. "I should have known better than to talk to you while you were photographing the kids."

"It's okay, really." Normally Mandy wasn't affected at all by conversation while she worked. There was plenty of background noise at the park, and none of that disturbed her concentration. But Jessica's statement had been far from typical conversation.

"Oh, no," Lainey said, her tiny brows furrowing when she accidentally unhooked one of her buckles.

Nathan turned back toward his little sister. "Here, Lainey, I'll help you." He guided her small hand through the process of fastening the strap while she watched in awe.

"Thanks, Bubba," she said, giving him a full baby-teeth smile.

Mandy snapped away, capturing the precious gesture and getting even better photographs than she'd planned.

"Oh, wasn't that adorable? Did you get that?" Jessica asked.

"I sure did," she said, grinning.

"Chad's going to love photos of the kids for his birthday present."

"I certainly hope so," Mandy said, while

a tiny poke in her back told her Kaden's patience had run out.

"Hey, Aunt Mandy, are you done yet?" Sky-blue eyes—Brantley blue eyes—squinted up at her in the sun.

"I am now," she said, packing up her camera. "Thank you for being so good while I took the pictures." She ran a hand over his sandy waves.

"So we can go play now?"

"Sure."

Kaden pumped a fist in the air. "Yes!" He ran toward Nathan. "You want to slide or swing?"

"We'll slide first, and then we'll swing," Nathan said.

"Okay!"

Nathan, at seven, was three years older than Kaden and therefore "major cool" in her nephew's eyes. Mandy loved seeing him so excited, so happy. Nine months ago she'd worried that she'd never see that sweet smile again, but there it was, stretching from cheek to cheek as he ran after his new friend toward the wide red slide. Maybe she was getting a better handle on this parenthood thing than she thought.

Jessica scooped up Lainey from Mandy's

hay props and kissed her soft blond curls. "I'm so glad you brought Kaden along today so he and Nathan can play."

"Me, too," Mandy said. It wasn't as if she really had a choice, since he was with her 24/7, but she didn't mind.

"Kaden looks like he's doing well." Jessica didn't add, "considering all that he's been through," but it was definitely implied.

"He is. It took a little time for him to get adjusted. He was quiet for a while, and he still asks a few questions about his mom and dad every now and then, but I really think he's going to be okay." Mandy wasn't so sure about herself, but she was determined that one way or another, Kaden would be fine. That was her main mission in life now, keeping her promise to Mia and making sure Kaden was okay.

"He sure enjoys playing with Nathan." Jessica pointed to him as he flew down the slide headfirst with his new friend cheering him on. "Nathan likes being the big boy. He's really good with younger kids and a great big brother for Lainey."

"I'm glad Kaden's getting a chance to play with another boy. Most of his time is spent with me." And soon Kaden's time would be split between Mandy and Daniel Brantley, if Daniel had his way and sent her packing.

Not happening.

"Hey, we have a great four-year-old class at the daycare if you ever want to bring him in and let him try it out. He wouldn't have to go full time, you know. There's a Mommy's Day Out program on Wednesday morning that you could put him in. It'd be good for him, social interaction and all."

Mandy blinked past the automatic response to the mommy reference. She wasn't Kaden's mommy. In fact, she missed his mommy, probably as much as Kaden. Mia had been more than a sister. She'd been Mandy's best friend and confidante. They'd been through so much together. Mia was truly the only person who not only knew Mandy's history but had experienced it, too.

"Sorry," Jessica said, obviously noticing the change in Mandy's disposition. "I'm sure you want to keep him close by with everything he's gone through. It's a reflex, telling people about the daycare, since I work there. But I wasn't thinking."

"It's fine." Mandy was glad so many people in town were interested in Kaden's well-being, a sign of how much Mia and Jacob had been loved and a promise that Mandy wasn't completely on her own raising her nephew. Claremont, Alabama, was small enough that everyone knew everybody's business and looked out for each other. Growing up, Mandy had hated that. Now, though, with Kaden to watch after, it didn't seem like such a bad thing. "From the looks of the way he and Nathan are playing, Kaden might enjoy spending time with other kids. I'll think about the Wednesday morning option."

"Well, I have it on good authority that the teacher for that four-year-old class would absolutely adore him."

"I'm guessing that teacher would be you?" Mandy asked.

"You'd guess right," Jessica said with a laugh.

"I swing, Mommy?" Lainey pointed toward the swing set beside the big slide where Nathan and Kaden were playing. "Please?"

"Sure."

They walked toward the swings chatting, and Jessica slowly worked her way into a topic that had come up way too often in Mandy's conversations around town over the past nine months.

"So, Chad told me about a new support

group at the community college for people who have been affected by drunk drivers, specifically those who have lost someone due to an accident caused by drunk driving." Jessica gazed at her friend, concern evident in her eyes. "I was thinking that maybe you could give it a try."

Mandy bit her lower lip and focused on Kaden, instantly orphaned when a drunk guy climbed behind the wheel, drove the wrong way and crashed head-on into Jacob and Mia's car. She swallowed past her emotion and said, "I don't need a support group."

"It might help," Jessica said. "I can tell you're coping okay, but I also can tell that you aren't as involved around town as you used to be. We've missed you at the church, you know. And I—well, everyone, really—wants to see you happy again."

"I'm happy with Kaden," she said truthfully, which was why she wasn't about to let Daniel take her nephew.

"I believe that, but you need to find happiness with life again. Most people can't relate to what you went through, but this group can. That's what they are there for."

Mandy pictured Mia, squeezing her hand as her life slipped away that night. Jacob had died at the scene, and the guy driving the other car died en route to the hospital, but Mia had held on until Mandy and Kaden made it to the hospital. Long enough for Mandy to get there and make that promise.

She kept her emotions in check as she glanced at Jessica, who was only trying to help. "I appreciate what you're trying to do, but I'm not ready to meet a group of people who've been through the same experience. It hurts to even think that someone else has had to suffer that much." She shook her head and added, "I don't think I'll ever be ready for a support group."

Jessica was undeterred. "Chad plans on talking to Daniel about going to the meetings also. Maybe it would be easier for you if y'all went together, especially since you were both affected by the same accident." She pushed Lainey in the toddler swing and waited for Mandy to respond.

Mandy was glad the boys were so involved with sliding that they weren't listening to this part of their conversation. She did her best to keep Kaden focused on the positive memories of his parents when they were alive, instead of the negative memory of their death.

"What do you think?" Jessica asked.

Mandy wasn't about to give her friend false hope. If Daniel was going, she sure wouldn't be a part of the group. He was only returning to Claremont to take Kaden, and she wasn't spending any more time with him than necessary. So she sat on a nearby swing, avoided the question and asked another one that would turn the subject back to what she most needed to know. "Did you say Daniel is already back?"

Jessica didn't press the issue, but instead nodded while Lainey pumped her feet and squealed with each push. "Yeah, I thought so, but I guess if you haven't seen him yet, he may not have made it back to Claremont, huh? I mean, I'm sure he'll make a beeline to come see Kaden, don't you think?"

Daniel would make a beeline to Kaden, not to Mandy. Miraculously, Mandy managed a smile. "Yes, I'm sure he will."

All of a sudden, Jessica slapped a hand over her mouth. "Oh, dear, maybe he was going to surprise you and Kaden, and I just blew it."

"No, really. It's fine." Mandy's shoes dug deeper in the dirt. "When I see him, I'll act surprised. Don't worry about it." But Mandy was definitely worried. Daniel could take

Kaden away from her, or try to take him away. She loved that little boy as if he were her own. Why couldn't Daniel see that?

Because of that email, her mind whispered.

"Well, that's what the church bulletin said on Sunday, that he was moving back this week and would begin working with the youth at the church as soon as he returned. I have to tell you, Chad and I were thrilled to hear he'd taken the youth minister job." Jessica smiled warmly. "It'll be nice seeing Nathan and Lainey become more involved with the youth group as they get older, especially if Daniel is leading the way."

"He's always been good with kids," Mandy mumbled, more to herself than to Jessica. Daniel worked directly with children in his missions; she'd seen the photos. Children beaming. Daniel laughing. If those photos were shown in court, a judge would probably decide that he'd be a better parent than Mandy. Her heart sputtered in her chest.

"There was a photo of Daniel in the church bulletin beside the announcement," Jessica continued. "It's always a bit of a jolt to see him and realize Jacob is gone. They looked so much alike, didn't they?"

Daniel's eyes were a brighter blue, in Mandy's opinion, but she didn't say so now. She simply nodded then glanced at Kaden, whose eyes were the exact same Caribbean shade. As a photographer, she prayed for that exact color of sky when she took photos outdoors. Bright, clear and beautiful. Breathtaking.

Kaden looked at her with those exquisite eyes and grinned. "Did you see me that time, Aunt Mandy? I went fast, didn't I?"

She swallowed. "Yes, you did."

He nodded. "Yep, I did." Then he ran back to the ladder to give the slide another go.

"You know, Chad and Daniel were really close in high school, back when they played baseball together. And Chad always thought the world of Daniel."

"I remember." Everyone thought the world of Daniel, even Mandy. In fact, she'd thought enough of him to propose to him when she was seventeen. She nodded absently while Jessica continued talking, and while her mind processed the facts. Daniel Brantley, Kaden's uncle, had taken the youth minister job. She'd told him when he came back home for that interview at the church that he didn't need to leave his mission work because of her impulsive email. She'd insisted that she never should have sent the thing and that she regretted hitting the *send* button the minute she clicked the mouse. But he'd pronounced he was coming back. No discussion. Riding in to save the day…and save Kaden from Mandy.

"And it'll really be something for him to tell the kids all about his mission work, especially about everything in Africa," Jessica continued. "You should have seen the slideshow they did last year when we had the annual appeal for the churches he started in Malawi and Tanzania. Seeing those people holding hands and moving into that water to be baptized, it touched my heart."

"Oh, I remember that! I liked the elephants," Nathan said, following Kaden down the slide.

Instead of running around to slide again, Kaden stopped, dusted off the knees of his jeans and peered at Nathan. "Uncle Daniel's elephants?" he asked.

Nathan shrugged. "I don't know. Is your uncle the guy from church who showed us the pictures of Africa and the elephants?"

Kaden looked to Mandy. "Is he talking about Uncle Daniel?"

"Yes, he is," Mandy said, still forcing a smile.

"Wow, *he's* your uncle? He's *so* cool!" Nathan said.

Kaden beamed. "Thanks!"

Yeah, thanks, Mandy thought dryly. The appeal Jessica referred to had been held the weekend of Kaden's fourth birthday last year. Daniel came home for his nephew's party and did a slideshow of his African missions at the church while he was in town. He didn't come home often and hadn't planned to return again for another year, but he'd ended up coming back two weeks later for Jacob's and Mia's funerals.

For the entire time that they remained at the park, Jessica talked nonstop, singing Daniel's praises and exclaiming about all of the wonderful advantages to having him back in town. Nathan joined in whenever he could, and Kaden automatically agreed with everything his older friend said. Mandy, on the other hand, spent her time wondering how quickly she could get him to leave. And exactly how long she had before she looked into another set of Brantley blue eyes, those belonging to the guy who broke her heart.

Chapter Two

Daniel Brantley never failed to appreciate the beauty of his hometown. No matter how many astounding landscapes he'd seen in his travels around the world, no matter the marvelous sights, smells and sounds of God's creation that he'd witnessed during his seven years in the mission field, Claremont always took his breath away.

Maybe it was the memory of being a kid and running these streets with Jacob, Chad, Mitch and the other guys from Claremont High…or maybe it was simply the picturesque beauty of the town nestled perfectly at the foot of Lookout Mountain in north Alabama. Daniel had no idea why, but he knew that in all of his twenty-eight years, in spite of how often he'd felt close to God in his travels, there was something about being home that made God even closer, close enough to touch.

He cranked the window down and inhaled the scents of early spring, flowers blooming, trees budding. Honeysuckle and gardenia mixed and mingled, their sweet scents lingering on the air and showcasing the fact that he was no longer in Africa.

He was home.

Nearing the road leading to the high school, he saw two rows of Bradford pear trees covered in stark white blooms lining the path to the school's entrance. Those blooms used to fall like snow all over this old red truck every spring a decade ago.

Glancing toward the brick buildings, he saw a bounty of teenagers' cars parked in the gravel lots on both sides. He and Jacob parked out there back in the day. They'd ridden to Claremont High together every morning, stayed after school for football practice in the fall, basketball practice in the winter and finally baseball, which had been the favorite sport for both Brantley boys, every spring.

The Brantley boys. The Brantley twins. The Brantley brood. They'd been dubbed lots of things back then, but no matter how the townsfolk referred to them, it'd never been individually. They'd always been a pair, and in spite of their differences, they'd liked it that way.

Daniel sighed. Would he ever get used to the fact that Jacob was gone? And didn't it seem odd that he'd been the one to venture out into more than his share of dangerous circumstances in his attempt to follow their missionary parents into the world and preach the Gospel, and yet the son that stayed home lost his life?

He pondered that irony as he drove through town. After Brother Henry told him to take his first day back to "get reacquainted with Claremont," Daniel had headed directly to the photography studio in the town square to find Mandy Carter and see Kaden. Yes, he loved his hometown, but he'd have never returned this soon if it hadn't been for his nephew. Unfortunately, he hadn't found Mandy or Kaden at Carter Photography. Instead, he found a hand-painted sign on the door.

On a photo shoot. Be back later.

And wasn't that just like Mandy? Be back later. No promises, nothing definite. Expecting the entire world to cater to her plans, her desires, the same way she had so many years ago. Some things never changed.

But Daniel wasn't going to simply sit outside her door and wait for her to show. Instead, he drove through town enjoying the gorgeous day and taking in the scenery while thinking about Kaden. A little boy needed a man in his life. In truth, a little boy needed a *dad* in his life.

Daniel had originally thought it was fine to stay in the mission field and let Mandy Carter raise his nephew. Daniel's parents had also agreed that Mandy was perfect for raising their grandson. Their commitment to the mission work in India kept them away, and while they loved the country there, they didn't think they should move Kaden away from the only home he'd ever known right after losing both of his parents. And they all agreed that Mandy adored Kaden and wanted to take care of her nephew.

"I love Claremont, and I love Kaden. Let him stay here with me, please. It's what Mia wanted."

Maybe because he'd been so upset over losing Jacob, Daniel had agreed. He couldn't wait to get back to Malawi to pray, to work and to grieve. After a few months, however, he realized that he couldn't get his nephew off his mind. And when he prayed to God to help him know what he should do about Kaden, he'd received that email from Mandy.

After reading what she'd written, he realized that Mandy was still the spoiled little princess she was way back then. Why he'd believed her when she said she wanted to make a life in Claremont and raise Kaden was beyond him. If Kaden was going to have the life Jacob and Mia had planned for him, it'd be Daniel who provided it. Certainly not Mandy Carter.

He continued driving toward the edge of town so he could see the new neighborhoods everyone was talking about, but before he reached the entrances to the subdivisions that had replaced the cotton fields, something caught his eye. Or rather, *someone* caught his eye.

A woman stood beside a blue pickup truck waving her hands in the air. Her sleeveless pink shirt was tied in a knot at her waist, and a turquoise scarf had been threaded through the belt loops of rolled up jeans. The ends of the scarf were tipped in sparkling stones that appeared to match the bejeweled sandals on her feet. She looked like a modern princess

Jasmine, waiting for Aladdin to scoop her up on a magic carpet and whisk her away from this "horrid little town," as she'd dubbed Claremont so many years ago.

While she waved him down, a thick pony-tail of shiny, chocolate-brown hair whipped across her face in the March breeze. But regardless of the mass of hair that made her face play peekaboo with Daniel as he approached, he had no doubt to the identity of the woman.

"Have mercy, Lord. Do You have to let her keep getting prettier?" His heart bumped solidly in his chest, the way it always did when he encountered the beauty that was Mandy Carter.

Daniel slowed the car as he neared and watched as one hand moved to shield her eyes from her hair, and her mouth formed a silent "Oh." Which was quickly followed by "No." Her wide smile slid into a flat line and she looked at him the same way she had practically every time he'd seen her in the past seven years, since that night he'd turned her down and walked away.

"You have anyone else in that old truck?" Mandy asked. "Someone who might actually be interested in helping me, perhaps?"

Here we go again. He grinned. "Afraid not."

He heard her grumble something and was pretty sure it included, "Should've recognized that truck," and "Why don't you drive away, you always do." But before he could respond, another voice joined in.

"Uncle Daniel?" Kaden called from her truck.

Daniel's heart leaped at the sound, and his smile widened. "That you in there, slugger?"

"Uncle Daniel! Hey, you're back!"

Oh, how he loved that boy. "Yes, I am, and I'm so glad I found you," Daniel said, leaning his head out the window as he spoke. "Let me pull the truck over, and I'll help you and Aunt Mandy." He was still in the middle of the street, and even though there wasn't a sign of another car around, he figured he should probably be safe.

He parked, then climbed out of the truck and walked to Kaden's side of the vehicle. He was anxious to hug his nephew, and he could do that while figuring out Mandy's problem with the truck.

"Uncle Daniel, my new friend Nathan said you're cool. He was talking about you and the elephants and stuff," Kaden said, climbing from his car seat and jumping into Daniel's arms.

"Nathan?" Daniel asked, holding his nephew tight.

"Chad and Jessica Martin's son." Mandy didn't look at Daniel as she spoke. Instead, she peered down the road as though she could will another car into existence.

"Right, I remember him. And he has a little sister, too, doesn't he?" Daniel asked Kaden, since he seemed to be the only one interested in conversing.

"Uh-huh, Lainey. She's little, only two."

Mandy cleared her throat. "I did a photo shoot at Hydrangea Park of Chad and Jessica's kids, and after the shoot, we stayed awhile to let Kaden play with Nathan." She'd apparently given up on anyone else coming to her rescue and was now more interested in the dirt around her feet than looking at Daniel.

"And then we got in the truck to go back home but we ran out of gas," Kaden said.

"Out of gas?" Daniel asked, smiling down at his nephew.

Mandy's head snapped up. "Yes, out of gas." Then she moved to the back of her truck, climbed into the bed and stepped around bales of hay and potted plants, searching for something. "I used the truck today because I needed some props, and I hardly ever drive granddaddy's old truck, so I forgot to check the tank," she said, shoving a hay bale aside. "Apparently, it was close to empty."

"Apparently," Daniel said, watching her push a few boxes, a shovel, an old-fashioned tricycle and some other odd, colorful objects around before withdrawing a small orange gas can.

"There," she said, pushing dark bangs out of her eyes as she worked her way through the maze of objects to reach the back of the truck. Then she jumped down with the orange can in hand. "We need a ride to the gas station, if you don't mind."

"And you'll need a ride back to your truck," Daniel said, uncertain why he found it so much fun to push her buttons.

"Yes, that, too. I thought someone from town would probably drive by soon and give us a ride, but if you could do it, that will work."

"I *am* from town," he reminded, "and it isn't a problem." He put Kaden on the ground beside him and ruffled his hair. "Come on, we'll move your car seat over to my truck."

"He likes to call it a booster seat," Mandy said. "Car seats are for babies, according to Kaden."

Kaden gave her a toothy grin then smiled even bigger for Daniel. "I guess it's both."

Mandy's face dropped. Daniel noticed, but had the wherewithal not to mention it. He really didn't want to participate in a contest of who Kaden liked better. He wanted Kaden happy. Period.

Within minutes, he'd moved the booster seat over and buckled Kaden into the extended cab, then opened the passenger door for Mandy.

She maintained her distance as she climbed in, but the breeze still sent a hint of her peach shampoo, or perfume, across Daniel's senses. He hadn't smelled anything quite like it in a long time, especially not in Malawi or Tanzania, that's for sure.

"When'd you get back from Africa?" Kaden asked.

"Late last night," Daniel said, closing Mandy's door and then walking around to his side of the truck and climbing in. "But I'm back to stay this time."

"Yes!" Kaden's excited yell from the backseat sent Daniel's spirits soaring. He'd made the right decision to come back home. *Thanks, God, for steering me once more.*

Mandy huffed out an exasperated breath.

And if You don't mind, Lord. Steer me again in how to handle Mandy.

"So we can spend time together whenever you want," Daniel continued, then glanced at Mandy. "I'm assuming that will be okay with you." Mandy had obtained custody after Mia and Jacob's accident. At the time she'd promised Daniel could see his nephew as often as he wanted, but she'd also thought he didn't plan on coming to Claremont more than twice a year at the max. "That is okay with you, isn't it, Mandy?" Daniel repeated.

Instead of answering, she reached over and flipped on the radio, which Daniel naturally had programmed to the contemporary Christian station. "Avalanche" by Manifest belted from the speakers, and Kaden immediately started tapping his hands against the booster seat with the upbeat sound.

Mandy looked at Kaden and verified that he was absorbed in the music then she leaned toward Daniel. "I asked you not to come back," she whispered.

"Yes, you did," he acknowledged, starting the truck.

"But you came, anyway."

"Yep, I did." He headed toward Bo Taylor's gas station a couple of miles toward town.

"Why?"

Daniel glanced in the rearview mirror at Kaden, now bobbing his head to the beat and attempting to sing along. Then he lowered his voice to match hers. "Because you also told me that I was out gallivanting across the globe and enjoying myself while you were left home to raise my nephew. You said that you were tired of having the weight of the world on your shoulders, so I came home to take that tiny weight off your hands and let you do what you want, Mandy." He nodded, sent a smile to Kaden via the rearview mirror. "We'll get everything settled with the court for custody and all, and then you can leave. It'll be the same as before, but in reverse. You can see the world yourself, and let me raise Kaden. Of course, you can come home and visit Kaden whenever you like. I promise to take very good care of him, the way Mia and Jacob would've wanted."

"I told you I shouldn't have sent that email. Do you have any idea what I had been through at that point?"

Daniel noticed Kaden's head had tilted and that he peered toward the front seat.

"Do you like this song, too, Uncle Daniel?"

"I sure do," Daniel said, smiling back and tapping his hands against the steering wheel with the beat. Then he glanced at Mandy. "We'll talk about this later."

"Fine."

He pulled into the station and saw Bo and Maura Taylor inside the store. He'd known Bo for years, but had just met Maura when he'd come to town for the interview with Brother Henry. She was talking to a customer at the register inside, but Bo walked out of the station and greeted them, and again Daniel sensed that familiarity of being back home, where everyone knows you and everyone cares. It was similar to the friendships he had with the tiny church groups he'd started in Malawi and Tanzania, but different because the people of Claremont had known him and his family for years. And they knew about him losing Jacob, not only his twin brother but unquestionably his best friend.

"Daniel, good to see you! I heard on Sunday that you took the job at the church. Sure is great to have you back," Bo said.

"It's good to be back."

"Need a fill up?"

"Sure, but I can get it," Daniel said, climbing out.

"This is full service, you know," Bo said. "And I enjoy doing my job."

"Okay, then, it's all yours," he said, sliding his seat forward so he could reach through and unbuckle Kaden. "You want to go get a snack and a drink inside?"

"Definitely!" Kaden scurried across the seat and climbed out.

"How about you, Mandy? Want anything?"

"No." She was still pouting, and Daniel let her, not that he really had a choice. But he hadn't told her anything that wasn't the truth about what she'd said in that email, and he knew that was her true feelings coming out. She felt trapped here, and he was going to set her free.

"I've got a can in the back that needs filling, too," he said to Bo.

"We ran out of gas," Kaden said, and Daniel caught Mandy's arms folding tightly against her chest with his proclamation.

"Who did?" Bo asked then peered into the truck. "Well, hey, Mandy. Didn't recognize you at first. Your hair's longer than I remember. It's been awhile."

"Hello, Mr. Taylor. Good to see you." She was polite but reserved, not the feisty, bubbly Mandy Carter that Daniel remembered, but then again, she was peeved.

The other customer left, and Maura came out of the gas station to visit, as well.

"You've met my wife, Maura, haven't you?" Bo asked.

"Yes," Daniel said. "Nice to see you again."

"Likewise," she said, smiling as Bo draped an arm around his wife. "I remember meeting you at the dinner on the grounds, right?"

"Yes, ma'am."

"And now you're going to be working at the church, I understand?"

"Yes, ma'am, with the youth."

"Well, that's great," she said. "Autumn, our granddaughter, is seven now and starting to get involved in the youth activities at the church. I'm glad to know you'll be working with that great group of kids."

"Maura and I married a month ago," Bo said. "Didn't know if you knew that."

"Brother Henry has been emailing the church bulletins to me each week while I've been gone, so I've stayed aware of my church family here," Daniel said. "Congratulations on the wedding."

"And who is this?" Maura asked, smiling at Kaden.

"This is my nephew, Kaden Brantley."

Bo glanced at Maura and gave her a slight nod, then a sympathetic smile toward Kaden, and Daniel knew that Bo had apparently told her about Mia and Jacob. Or she could have heard it from someone at church. It was pretty big news in a small town when anyone died, but in this case even more because Mia and Jacob were so young and had so much to live for, particularly Kaden.

Maura's mouth tightened, and she blinked a couple of times then squatted down to eye level with Kaden. "You know what, I made some cookies earlier to sell inside, but I haven't had anyone here to taste them and let me know if they're okay. Would you want to do that for me?"

"Would I! Yes, ma'am!"

Maura held out a hand, and Kaden took it. Then she turned toward Daniel's door, still open, to see Mandy sitting inside. "Would you like to come in, too?"

"We're going to try cookies, Aunt Mandy," Kaden said. "Come on. You love cookies!"

"They're fresh baked," Maura tempted.

Mandy smiled—something Daniel certainly hadn't seen since his arrival—and then climbed out of the passenger side. "I can't imagine turning down fresh-baked cookies."

"Aunt Mandy really likes cookies. We make them itchy."

"Itchy?" Maura asked.

Mandy laughed, and Daniel was absorbed in the fullness of the sound, rolling out effortlessly, as though she liked nothing better than to set it free. Daniel was grateful that Kaden had undoubtedly been witness to it, because he laughed along with her now.

"Wh-what?" Kaden giggled. "What'd I say?"

"We make them from scratch," Mandy told him, rubbing her hand over his head affectionately. "We don't make them itchy."

Bo, Maura and Daniel all chuckled along.

"But that was close," Mandy finally said.

Kaden grinned. "Thanks!"

When their laughter subsided, Maura nodded toward Mandy. "Okay, let's go test some of those cookies." They turned and started toward the small gas station. Maura wiped a couple of laugh tears from her cheeks and then directed her attention on Mandy. "I don't believe we've met, have we?"

"I don't think so. I'm Mandy Carter,

Kaden's aunt. I own the photography store in the town square. Well, I do now. It belonged to my grandparents and then my sister." Her voice trailed off. "Now just me."

"And me. I help," Kaden said. "And we live there, at the top of the store."

"Yes, Kaden definitely helps," Mandy said.

Daniel waited until they entered the station. "I'm a little surprised that Maura has never met Mandy."

"I'm trying to introduce her to everyone in town, but I suppose our paths haven't crossed with Mandy's too much. We do go to the town square a bit. Autumn enjoys going to the toy shop and Nelson's five-and-dime, but we haven't been in the photography shop." He smiled broadly. "Need to get over there. Maura and I don't have a lot of photos of us together, other than the wedding, you know."

"I'm guessing you'd have seen Mandy if she'd been at church?"

Bo frowned. "You know the answer to that. Everyone sees everyone at church. But no, she hasn't been there, not since Mia and Jacob's accident. And truthfully, Mandy never was much for church, from what I remember. She was in the same grade as my daughter Hannah, you know, but seems like when Hannah got more involved in church during those later teen years, Mandy kind of pulled away."

Daniel remembered that time in Mandy's life, and now he wished he'd have done something to bring her back to God.

Bo's eyes lifted. "But I will invite her today. Don't know why I didn't think about that sooner. I went years away from God, you know, and it's not a fun place to be, away from Him." He paused. "Maura, too, after she lost her daughter. I think that's why she's probably going to bond pretty well with that little Kaden. Our granddaughter, Autumn, lost her mother. But Autumn is doing great now. She's a little older than Kaden, but I'm sure they'd get along real well. Maybe if you can get Mandy to bring him to church, he and Autumn can meet there."

"Kaden will come to church with me," Daniel said. There was no question that he'd take his nephew back to church, but if he had his way, he'd bring Mandy back to God, too. If she was going off to see the world, and Daniel was determined to let her go, he wanted to know she had God along for the trip.

"Well, it'll be good for Kaden to have both

of you in his life," Bo said. "A child needs that, people who care and are working together for his or her best interest. Family. People who love each other."

Daniel couldn't offer all of that, not when it came to him and Mandy, but they did both care about Kaden. He glanced up to see Maura, Mandy and Kaden exit the store. Kaden had a chocolate chip cookie in one hand and a carton of milk in the other. Mandy's hands were filled with the same, and so were Maura's.

"You didn't bring us any?" Bo teased.

"Our hands were full," Kaden said, using his tongue to grab a bit of stray chocolate from his lip, "but yours are waiting for you on the counter."

Mandy grinned and licked the chocolate from her fingers. She looked so different when she smiled, actually sweet, like someone Daniel could actually connect with. And Daniel suddenly noticed that he'd just seen that same smile on Kaden. He looked to his nephew, then back to Mandy. Kaden had Mandy's smile.

"You okay, Uncle Daniel?" Kaden asked, and Daniel wondered if his thoughts were that obvious.

Kaden had *his* eyes and *Mandy's* smile. That was so noticeable now, and Daniel wondered why. *God, what are you telling me?*

"Uncle Daniel?" Kaden repeated.

Daniel cleared his throat. "I'm fine," he answered.

"He's wanting some of those cookies," Bo said to Kaden.

Daniel grinned. "I sure do. Here you go," he handed over several bills to Bo, "for the gas, the milk and the cookies."

"I'll bring your change for the gas. The milk and cookies are on the house. We'll consider it your welcome home treat. And I'll grab your cookies when I come back out with your change," Bo said, walking toward the station.

"Can I have another cookie please?" Kaden asked.

"Sure," Maura said. "Come on, I'll take you to get one."

She and Kaden followed Bo, and Daniel found himself alone with Mandy. She'd finished her cookie and held tightly to her small carton of milk while she leaned against the truck and avoided looking in Daniel's direction. He took a deep breath and decided he might as well get everything out in the open while he had the chance.

"I want you to give me custody," he said. "After the funerals, it seemed like a good idea for you to raise Kaden, but I didn't consider the fact that you want to see the world. And I'm good with that. I've had my chance to travel. Now I want to work here with the church, and I want to raise Kaden."

She shifted, turned dark eyes toward Daniel. "Listen, I wish you'd believe me. I didn't mean what I said in that email. Kaden had been throwing up for three days straight and was burning up with fever. I was tired from puke patrol and was catching that wretched bug myself." She sighed heavily. "When I sent the email, I already had a fever and had gotten sick twice myself. It was a weak moment, and I sent you a second email the next morning to let you know I didn't mean it."

"But I'd already emailed Brother Henry asking for a job."

"So you could have told him you changed your mind."

"But I didn't." He put the gas can in the back of the truck. "Mandy, I'm the same guy who heard you say nearly those exact words seven years ago, that you would do anything to leave this horrid little town."

"I can't believe you'd bring that up now. Do you really think I meant it? That I would have *married you* just to get away from here?"

"Yes, Mandy, I do."

She opened her mouth and then snapped it shut when Kaden ran out of the store in front of Bo and Maura.

"Here's yours," he said, handing Daniel a carton of milk and a small brown bag. "Mrs. Maura gave you three cookies, 'cause she said men eat more than boys. But then she gave me another one, so I got three, too."

"Guess you're a man," Daniel said, patting Kaden's back.

"Yep," Kaden said, shimmying into the backseat. "Guess so."

"Well, I suppose we'll see you again in a few minutes," Bo said to Mandy. "You'll need gas in your car, right?"

"That's right," she said. "Thank you for the cookies and milk."

"You're welcome." He grinned. "And Mandy, we'd love to have you back at church, you know."

She returned the smile, but this time it didn't reach her eyes. "I know. Thank you."

Then she got in the passenger seat and buckled up.

"Aunt Mandy?"

"Yes?"

"Can I stay in this truck till we get home?"

Daniel paused climbing in to see what
she'd say.

Mandy swallowed then turned warm eyes
toward Kaden. "If you want to, that's fine.
You haven't seen Uncle Daniel in a while.
You probably want to visit and ask him about
those elephants, don't you?"

Kaden took a sip of milk from his carton,
wiped his mouth with the back of his hand.
"Yeah, maybe. But I mainly want to stay in
this truck because it was Daddy's. We always
went riding in this truck, before Mommy and
Daddy went to heaven."

Chapter Three

After getting Mandy's truck running again, Daniel followed her back to the gas station. Bo saw them and walked out of the station looking glad. Daniel had planned to wait until she filled up and then follow her home, but Mandy got out of her truck and walked back to his with a keychain dangling from her hand. Daniel noticed a rectangular photo suspended from the silver ring, and as she got closer the image came into focus and displayed Mandy and Mia on Mia's wedding day.

She neared his open window and handed him the keychain. The close proximity sent another sweet fragrance of peaches teasing Daniel's senses, and he swallowed past the urge to inhale deeper.

"Here's the key to the shop. You can go

on ahead and spend a little time with Kaden until I get there." She peeked toward the backseat and displayed another beautiful smile that wasn't at all intended for Daniel's enjoyment.

But he enjoyed it, anyway.

"Kaden, maybe you can show Uncle Daniel that house we built last night. That sound good to you?"

"Sure!"

"Lincoln Logs," she said to Daniel. Her words were still short toward him, but he was growing used to it. She'd been perfecting her stoicism around him for seven years, after all.

"Those were mine and Jacob's favorite toys growing up," Daniel said quietly.

A look passed over her face, and he figured she was trying to decide whether to respond or simply walk away. Then her mouth slid to the side, and she blinked a couple of times before whispering softly enough for Kaden not to hear, "I remembered Mia had planned to get him some for Christmas so I asked Mr. Tolleson at Nelson's if he could order a set. They came in yesterday." She swallowed. "We played with them last night until we were both ready for bed, but I'm guessing he would probably like a guy to help with the building. I do my best, but I'm still learning."

Daniel noticed that her eyes glistened. Undoubtedly she'd been crying during the short drive from where they'd picked up her car to the station. And Daniel understood. Kaden's comment about "before Mommy and Daddy went to heaven," was a sharp reminder that his nephew's life had been forever altered by a distinctive barrier. In fact, all three of their lives had been altered by that same barrier. The time before Mia and Jacob died, and the time after.

Mandy exhaled thickly and said to Kaden, "I'll see you back at home, okay?"

"Okay," he said, rummaging through the brown bag Maura had given him earlier and pulling out another cookie.

"Hey, don't eat too many. You'll ruin your dinner," she warned. "I made that taco soup you wanted."

"I've just got this one left," Kaden said, taking a bite. "And I've only had three, same as Uncle Daniel."

"Okay. I will see both of you at home, then." She turned and walked toward Bo.

Daniel drove to the town square thinking about Mandy, the way she spoke to him and more importantly the way she spoke to Kaden. There had been an intimacy there that he hadn't anticipated, a maternal aspect to her tone and to her words.

By the time they arrived at the photo shop, Kaden had told Daniel about how he and Mandy built the big house out of logs, how they had picnics at the park and how she was trying to help him ride a big boy bike, but she hadn't let go of the back yet, even though he really *really* wanted her to.

"She keeps running behind me 'cause she don't want me to fall," Kaden said, standing beside Daniel as he turned the key in the lock of the shop's door.

"She's just trying to keep you from getting hurt," Daniel explained.

"But how'm I gonna ride by myself if she won't let go?"

"Maybe she'll let me help you learn," Daniel offered.

"You're gonna let go?"

"Yes," Daniel promised. Undoubtedly Kaden would take a few falls, probably the exact reason Mandy didn't want to let go. He'd been hurt enough, and she didn't want it to happen again in any way, shape or form. Neither did Daniel. But Kaden had a point;

how would he learn, how would he grow, if everyone didn't "let go" every now and then?

Kaden pointed to the hand-painted sign on the door. "We're open for business now that we're back, so we have to flip it over."

Daniel's laugh came easy. "You really are Aunt Mandy's helper, aren't you?"

"Yep," Kaden said, leading the way through the gallery portion of the store. "She needs me. She says so all the time."

Something about the simple statement resonated with Daniel, but he didn't stop to analyze why. Instead, he followed his nephew through the abundance of photos covering the walls and easels inside Carter Photography. Striking pictures of babies, children, couples and families. There were still life photos, as well, stargazer lilies, an antique sewing machine, a bowl of peaches. But regardless of the subjects portrayed in each photograph, Mandy's work was incredible. He'd known her family was big into photography, but until this moment he hadn't realized that Mandy had inherited the talent.

"Come on and I'll show you our house we built last night," Kaden said, moving down a hallway and past two studio rooms with backdrops and props stuffed into every corner.

The hall was filled with senior portraits of kids from Claremont High, some in formal wear and others outdoors. Each photo captured the personality of the teen, whether a boy in his baseball or football uniform, or a girl in an evening gown. It wasn't what they were wearing but the way they looked that made the teens stand out, as though Mandy had depicted their very essence in the shot.

"Stunning," he said.

"It's upstairs," Kaden called, not hearing Daniel's comment and passing through the kitchen where a Crock-Pot held something that Daniel assumed was taco soup. The seasonings filled the air and caused his stomach to growl.

Kaden evidently heard. "Hey, you hungry?"

"It just smells good," Daniel said.

"Aunt Mandy cooks great," he said. "You staying to eat with us?"

Daniel inhaled another spicy whiff. "I certainly hope so," he said without thinking, then realized that Mandy would probably toss him out the door as soon as she returned. Or throw a little extra Tabasco in his bowl.

"Cool!" Kaden continued through the kitchen to start up a stairway lined with landscape photos.

Daniel surveyed these with equal interest. Several featured the heart-shaped pond at Hydrangea Park in the midst of the annual Valentine's display, pink lights and roses covering gazebos, the arched entrance and silhouettes of couples throughout. The Smoky Mountains, their dark heights capped with stark white snow and garnished with the pale gray clouds that earned their name. Again, beautiful and breathtaking. The last photo was a white sandy beach at dusk, a red-gold sun dipping in the distance and a little boy putting the finishing touches on an elaborate sandcastle complete with turrets, a moat and a bridge that appeared to be made out of Popsicle sticks.

Daniel stepped closer, because that little boy looked very familiar. "Kaden?"

Kaden had already topped the stairs, but started back down. "Yeah?"

"Is that you?" He pointed to the photo.

"Yep. Aunt Mandy took me to the beach and helped me build the best sandcastle in the world." He grinned, his pride shining through. "Then she took my picture for her contests."

"Her contests?"

"Yep. If she wins, she'll get in the big glammeries. That's her dream. Aunt Mandy says everybody's got dreams that they want, and she wants the glammeries. Not a little glammery, like hers, but really big glammeries."

"Glammeries?"

"Where they show her pictures for lots and lots of people," Kaden explained.

Daniel kept his laugh in check. "Galleries?"

"Yep, that's it," Kaden said, then turned, obviously anxious to get upstairs. "That's Aunt Mandy's dream. My dream is a secret, and Aunt Mandy says that's okay. I can keep it a secret if I want to."

Daniel instantly wondered what dream Kaden had, but he didn't ask. Instead, he answered, "Yes, you can." With each passing minute, he grew more and more touched by Kaden's relationship with Mandy. Why wouldn't she be content to raise this amazing kid? But he'd read that email, and even if it wasn't how she was feeling today, he believed that deep inside she still felt that Kaden was something of a burden. Daniel was certain that the email hadn't been a misinterpretation of her feelings. Not entirely, anyway.

"Come on, and I'll show you our house we made."

Growing up, Daniel had known that Mia and Mandy lived above the photo shop with their grandparents, but he'd never seen the upstairs portion until now. It was small but neat and filled with antique furniture and an abundance of photos.

Some of the pictures were older, obviously taken by Mandy's grandfather, the town's only photographer when Daniel had been younger. But when they entered Kaden's room, he found that his nephew's walls were filled with photos that had undoubtedly been taken by Mandy. Pictures of Mia and Jacob snuggling a baby Kaden. Mia kneeling behind Kaden as he learned to walk, his chubby arms reaching out toward Jacob and his excited grin stretching across his little face. Daniel viewed several more photos of the happy family at various stages of Jacob and Mia's four short years with Kaden, and then one more photo that caused Daniel pause.

Daniel and Jacob stood in the hospital hallway after Kaden's birth. Beside the nursery door, they draped arms around each other and punched opposite fists in the air as they cheered for the arrival of Jacob and Mia's beautiful baby boy. There were many pictures of the Brantley twins celebrating. Some were taken in end zones, others at home plate and others at center court. But none meant more to Daniel than this particular event.

He'd been so happy when Jacob had rushed from the delivery room to yell the news. A beautiful, healthy baby boy had joined the Brantley family. Daniel had looked forward to the day when Jacob would celebrate the birth of Daniel's firstborn in the same manner.

Now that would never happen.

His heart clenched in his chest. He remembered that moment when the photo had been taken like it was yesterday. Before now, he'd thought he only had the memory. He had no idea Mandy had captured it on film.

"That's you and Daddy," Kaden said. "You were happy."

He swallowed. "Yes, we sure were, because you were just born."

"I know," Kaden said matter-of-factly. "Aunt Mandy told me." He pointed to the other side of the room. "There it is. Cool, huh?"

Daniel turned to follow his finger and saw a table covered from one edge to the other with the most elaborate log cabin he'd ever seen. With three full levels, it took up the entire table.

"It's called a wilderness lodge," Kaden said. "That's what Aunt Mandy said. We found it in there." He pointed to a thick book in a wooden chair nearby.

Daniel picked up the book. "Building Dream Homes with Lincoln Logs," he read aloud.

"Yep," Kaden said. "Look, we've got a gate over here and a place for our animals, but we haven't bought animals yet. We were gonna make a barn for the animals, too, but we ran out of room, so Aunt Mandy has gotta get another table. Just a little one, since we're already using a bunch of space in here and this is where I like to play."

"I see." Daniel did see. There was only one wall in Kaden's room that wasn't graced with family photos, and that wall instead housed bookshelves that were the width and height of the entire wall.

And the shelves weren't empty. On the contrary, they were filled with all kinds of books on parenting; raising little boys; building sandcastles; playing baseball; learning to ride a bicycle; how to safely catch and raise frogs, turtles and lizards, and every other subject that might be appealing to a woman trying to raise a four-year-old boy. The bottom two shelves were filled with books for said boy, great bedtime stories. Daniel was thrilled to see that several of those books were Bible stories. *David and Goliath, Jonah and the Whale, Moses and the Ten Commandments.*

"Do you know where we can get the animals for the barn?" Kaden asked. "Aunt Mandy was going to take me to the store today after we went to the park, but then we ran out of gas. Do you know where to buy toy animals?"

"I'm not sure." Daniel assumed the Tiny Tots Treasure Box was still the place to go for toys on the square, but he wasn't certain whether Mr. Feazell carried the kind of animals Kaden would want for his wilderness lodge.

"That's okay. Aunt Mandy will know."

"Well, if she doesn't, I'm sure she'll find out," he said, still surprised at the amount of effort she was obviously putting into raising Kaden.

A bell echoed through the home, and Kaden took off toward the stairs. "Customers," he said. "Come on."

Daniel followed him as he barreled down

the stairs, through the kitchen and then through the studio-lined hallway to reach the main store.

"Oh, hey!" Kaden yelled.

"Well, hello," a woman's voice said.

Daniel caught up and rounded the corner to see Jessica Martin and her two children in the gallery. Her son stood by her side and her little girl slept sweetly on Jessica's shoulder with her thumb hanging from her mouth.

"Well, hey, Daniel. I asked Mandy earlier if you were back in town yet. I saw in the church bulletin on Sunday that you took the job as youth minister. Can't tell you how excited Chad and I were to see that."

"Thanks. I'm pretty excited myself. Glad to be back home, especially with Kaden here." He squeezed Kaden's shoulders.

Jessica glanced around the shop. "So, is Mandy here?"

"No, we ran out of gas, and Uncle Daniel helped us, but now she's getting the gas in the truck so she can come back here," Kaden said, visibly trying to sound like the knowledgeable "big boy" in front of Nathan, who nodded as though he were the only one needing an explanation.

"Well, I'm glad you were able to help." Jessica opened her purse and pulled out a card. "I remembered after we left that I didn't think to give Mandy my cell number. Since the photos are a surprise for Chad's birthday, I wanted to drop by and give it to her. Can you pass this on to her?"

"Sure," Daniel said, taking the card.

"You want to go see my log house?" Kaden asked Nathan. "Aunt Mandy got this book to show us how to make it. It's called a wilderness lodge, cause if it was real, it'd be in the wilderness. That's what Aunt Mandy said."

"Oh, that's so nice of you to ask, Kaden," Jessica said. "But I was about to head over to Scraps and Crafts to pick up a few things for the daycare. Maybe I can bring Nathan back sometime when he can play with you awhile, or maybe you could come over to our house and play sometime."

"Okay," Kaden said, his disappointment evident.

Jessica looked thoughtful. "You know, I'm going to be busy looking at things for the daycare, but Nathan will probably want to check out some of the toys she keeps at the back of the store. Would you like to come look at those with him?"

"Do you think they have farm animals?

I need some for my wilderness lodge," Kaden said.

"I don't know, but you could check and see," Jessica said.

Kaden turned to Daniel. "Can I go? Please?"

Daniel was taken aback at first that Kaden would ask his permission. He wasn't his parent or guardian. But he wanted to be, very much. And he couldn't deny that it felt good to have even a semblance of what that role would entail. "I think that'd be fine," he said.

"Cool!"

"We'll be back soon," Jessica said. "Twenty minutes tops."

"Sounds great," Daniel said, then caught Kaden's attention before he headed out the door. "Hey, Kaden, come here a minute."

Kaden darted back to Daniel with a questioning gaze. "Yes, sir?"

Have mercy, he was a sweet kid. "Here you go, in case you find some animals that will work for your lodge." He withdrew his wallet and pulled out a five.

"Wow, Uncle Daniel!" Kaden said, grinning. "Thanks!" Then he turned and joined Nathan near the door.

"We won't be long," Jessica repeated. "I still have to cook supper."

"Take your time," Daniel said, and moved to open the door so she could pass through with Lainey now softly snoring on her shoulder.

He watched them walk away, started back through the shop and heard a commotion in the back that he could only assume was the store's owner. Daniel calmly passed through the hall and beyond the two studios to the rear entrance behind the kitchen where, sure enough, Mandy threw her keys on a counter, dropped her purse and blew long dark bangs from her eyes. She looked up and announced, "I'm not leaving, Daniel."

Have mercy, she was even prettier when she was mad. "Well, fancy that, Mandy. Neither am I."

Chapter Four

Mandy's mind was made up, and there was nothing Daniel Brantley could do to change it. The entire drive from the gas station to the town square, Mia's words kept reverberating through her mind.

"Mandy, please, promise me. Take care of Kaden."

On that awful night in the emergency room before Mia's last breath, Mandy had made that promise, and since that night she'd done exactly that, she *had* taken care of Kaden. Then, because of one bad day and an impulsive email, Daniel thought he could traipse back into town and take over, discount everything she'd done right because of one little thing she did wrong.

Fixated on how bad a mistake it was to send that stupid email, Mandy had slammed the door, flung her keys and tossed her purse. Then she got that eerie sick feeling that someone was watching her, and she lost her breath. Then again, this was the same guy that had continually taken her breath away throughout middle school and high school. Back then it was because he was the most gorgeous guy she'd ever seen. Now it was because she was startled to find six feet of mostly muscled and quite magnificent male suddenly standing in the middle of her kitchen.

But there he stood, piercing blue eyes, sandy hair that was never fixed but always looked absolutely perfect, strong cheekbones and a mouth that seemed to harbor a perpetual semi smirk each and every time he looked at Mandy. Unquestionably still the most attractive man ever. She'd known he was here with Kaden, so it shouldn't have surprised her to run smack-dab into him when she entered the back of her home. But it did, and she had to concentrate to control her racing pulse.

Why did the entire package of Daniel Brantley still cause her knees to sway, even when he'd upset her enough to make her want to fling something at that beautifully chiseled face? He was a missionary that looked like a model, plain and simple. Who'd ever heard of such?

She'd anticipated his response the whole way over. "Okay, so now that we know neither of us is budging from Claremont, it all boils down to this. Kaden and I have been doing very well without you. I wish you would believe me, Daniel."

He gave her a look that said he was less than convinced.

She changed tactics. "Listen, I know how important your mission work is to you, and I know you'd planned to stay in Africa several more years. It makes me feel terrible—" she put a hand to her heart for emphasis "—absolutely terrible that my email caused you to leave that behind." She paused, shook her head, and repeated with as much emotion as she could muster, "Really, you didn't need to come back."

Come on, Daniel. It's the truth. Why can't you just believe me?

"But I'm here now, and I'm staying," he said flatly.

There was no point in arguing. Like her grandmother had always predicted, her impulsive nature was coming back to bite her in the behind. She *had* always wanted to leave Claremont and see the world, and Daniel knew it thanks to that impromptu proposal when she'd been seventeen. But that desire faded away the night Mia died. Now she wanted nothing more than to be a good mother figure to Kaden and stay put in Claremont.

Unfortunately that foolish email caused Daniel, the person who could most threaten her custody of Kaden, to believe otherwise.

"I'm staying, Mandy." His repeated words were deliberate and determined.

She refused to let him believe she would back down. "Then we need to come up with a compromise, because I promised Mia I'd take care of Kaden—and I'm not about to break that promise. I love him, and despite what I implied in that foolish email, I've never regretted being here with Kaden." She exhaled deeply. "Yes, I wanted to travel abroad and photograph the world, but I've learned that photography here can be equally challenging. Truth is, I really enjoy living in Claremont. I'm perfectly content to stay here permanently and raise Kaden the way Mia and Jacob wanted."

She wished it didn't sound so much like she was trying to convince herself instead of the stunning man standing in her kitchen. And did she have to always focus on how gorgeous he was? Or how manly he smelled, with that hint of crisp mint, or pine, or whatever it was.

Mandy, get a grip. He wants custody of Kaden, and you can't let that happen. Or lose your focus because he still happens to make you weak-kneed.

"I mean it, Daniel. I want to stay here. I want to raise Kaden. And I want to keep custody."

"I know," he said, no further explanation than that. He knew she wanted custody, but apparently he was going to try to get it, anyway. He calmly pulled out a chair and sat at the kitchen table as though he belonged here, in the middle of her home and in the middle of her life. And Mandy realized that if he was determined to stick around, then that's where he'd be, in the middle of her life from now on. Mandy Carter and Daniel Brantley, working together to raise a child. She'd had a vision, a dream, of something very similar to that a few years ago.

A shiver of apprehension shimmied down her spine at that awareness. Could she handle being around Daniel that much? And hearing him make little comments without explanation, like the one he'd just made? Back when she was in middle school and he was in high school, she'd been completely in awe by every statement that came out of that pretty mouth. She'd been too intimidated by the great Daniel Brantley to call him on any of his baffling remarks. *"You'll understand when you're older, Mandy."* She'd heard that from Daniel, Jacob—and even Mia—continually. And hated it each and every time. But that was when the four years age difference between them made her feel inferior. When she was twelve and they were sixteen, those years had been huge. But now that Daniel was twenty-eight and she twenty-four...not so much.

Daniel seemed all-knowing and all-powerful back then, like he'd experienced so much more than she ever had or ever would. But Mandy had also experienced plenty since that time. She'd lost almost everyone she cared about, and she'd survived. More than that, she'd kept a promise by taking care of the little boy that meant the world to her. So she was *not* intimidated by Daniel anymore. She knew that she was a good mother figure to Kaden. She simply had to figure out how to convince Daniel—and probably a judge—of that fact.

The reminder of her status as mom caused her to realize that she hadn't heard any movement upstairs since she'd entered the house. "Where's Kaden?" She sure didn't want him overhearing this conversation.

"Jessica Martin came by to bring you her cell number," Daniel said. "It's over there on the counter." He motioned to a small white card near the telephone. "And she invited Kaden to go to the craft store with her, Nathan and Lainey. I assumed it would be okay with you. *Is* it okay?"

She blinked, finding a modicum of pleasure that he was at least asking her approval, even if after the fact. "Yes, of course it's okay," she said. "I want him to make new friends, and he's really hit it off with Nathan."

Daniel nodded. "That's what I thought." He motioned to the chair across the table. "Mandy, since we've got a little time before Kaden comes back, let's talk about custody."

Her stomach pitched with the mention of the word, but she swallowed past the nauseous feeling, said, "Okay," and sat in the chair.

He clasped his hands in front of him, and

Mandy was drawn to the tan skin, the disarming masculinity that radiated from Daniel Brantley, even in the shape of his hands. Would the fact that he was male and could teach Kaden boy things better than Mandy play a factor in court, if they ended up in a war over custody? Did gender count in custody battles? Mandy had no clue. No one had ever fought for custody of her or Mia growing up. They were blessed that their grandparents wanted them. As far as their parents were concerned, they'd never known the identity of their father, and their mother had left Claremont right after Mandy's birth and never returned.

But Kaden wouldn't grow up thinking no one wanted him. Mandy wanted him, and she would fight for him starting right now. "I think we've established that I want custody, Daniel."

His mouth tightened then he nodded. "Mandy, I believe that you *think* you want to stay in Claremont and raise Kaden. But I also believe that there was a hint of truth in that email. Yes, you were having a bad day, but the words in that message were clearly coming from your desire to leave."

She blew out an exasperated breath. "I was

sick. I was exhausted. Everyone says things they don't mean when they're not feeling well, Daniel," she said, proud of herself for keeping her voice steady and calm when she really wanted to scream.

"That's probably true," he said. "But you've said the same thing before." Those blue eyes lifted to find hers and cast her right back to that night seven years ago when she'd begged him to marry her and take her away from her horrible, tiny hometown.

"I didn't mean it then, either," Mandy snapped and struggled not to flinch as she told the lie.

His eyes said he knew differently. "I want custody."

Mandy imagined the two of them in court pleading their cases for why they should raise Kaden. What court would give her custody over a missionary? Especially a missionary that had an email from her saying that she thought Kaden was a burden. But Daniel would never bring that email to court. Would he?

If he wanted Kaden that badly, he might. Mandy knew she would, if the tables were turned. That wave of nausea grew stronger.

She inhaled through her nose, focused on maintaining composure.

"You don't even know what it's like to raise a child," she said.

"And you do?"

"I've had more experience than you," she retorted, unable to control the defensive tone. Then she regrouped and asked, "How do you know that you even *want* to raise Kaden? You've seen him on visits and done things with him occasionally, but being with him day-to-day is totally different than being the visiting uncle. It's a *lot* of responsibility, and it *isn't* all fun and games." She realized that sounded negative. "But most of the time it's amazing," she added quickly. "I want to raise him, Daniel. I love being a mom—or mother figure—to him. I really do."

His full lip quirked to the side and then he nodded. "You know what, you have a point."

"I do?" she questioned, then amended with a slap of her palm on the table, "Yes, I do."

His jaw flexed, fighting back a grin. If he laughed at her now she just might have to hit him.

"Yes, you do," he repeated. "I haven't spent a lot of alone time with Kaden, and any judge will want to know whether he is comfortable with me as a parent figure. So why don't we give it a trial run? See if he'd like to spend some time with me, one-on-one? The house the church provided for me has three bedrooms, so I've got the room." He shrugged. "Who knows? You may be right. I may not be able to handle it."

"But," Mandy started, but for the life of her couldn't come up with an argument to keep Kaden from spending time with his uncle. Daniel had a right to that, after all, because that had been their original agreement when she'd gained custody. Daniel could spend time with Kaden whenever he was back in Claremont. However, she hadn't expected that to be more than a few days every year.

"But what?" he asked.

"For how long? How long do you want Kaden to stay with you?"

"I'm going to stay with Uncle Daniel?" Kaden's voice caused Mandy to jump in her chair, and she turned to see Jessica standing inside the open doorway between the hallway and the kitchen with Kaden and Nathan at her side and Lainey snoozing on her shoulder.

"I can't believe I didn't hear the doorbell," Mandy sputtered. She'd been so absorbed with the intense conversation with Daniel that she must have drowned out the normally noticeable sound.

"We waited up front for a moment but then Kaden led us on in. I hope that's okay," Jessica said, stroking Lainey's back.

"It's fine," Mandy said. "I just had a lot on my mind." A major understatement.

"Am I really going to stay with Uncle Daniel?" Kaden asked again. "Like today?"

Mandy's heart fell at his undeniable enthusiasm. "Would you like that, Kaden?" she asked, knowing the answer before he yelled out an exuberant, "Yes!"

She glanced to Daniel, smiling but not obnoxiously. He was happy, but he shot a look of pity toward Mandy that acknowledged he realized this wasn't easy.

"Probably not today," Daniel said. "I had planned to see about picking you and Aunt Mandy up for church tomorrow night, anyway. You could go home with me after church. That will give her a chance to get your things packed and ready to go. And then maybe you could stay with me until we all go back to church on Sunday morning?" Daniel glanced toward Mandy. "What do you think?"

"Oh, we'd love to have you back at church, Mandy," Jessica gushed.

Mandy was being ambushed, and she didn't appreciate it one bit. She wasn't ready to go back to church, wasn't ready to forgive God for what she'd been through over the past decade, losing every person who actually cared about her—every person, that is, except Kaden. Now Daniel was trying to take him *and* tie church into the deal? "I'm not going to church tomorrow night, but you can pick up Kaden and take him with you, if he would like to go."

"Cool!" Kaden exclaimed, and Mandy bit back the urge to cry.

She swallowed, continued, "But Little League sign-ups are Saturday. I wanted to be there for that, so why don't we meet back up at the Little League fields Saturday morning, and he can come back home with me after the sign-ups?" Her breathing began to steady as she realized that she had come up with a solution to give Daniel a little time with Kaden without requiring her to step one foot in the church.

"Aunt Mandy, Nathan asked me to come play at his house on Saturday. That's what I was coming to ask you about," Kaden said.

"After the sign-ups," Jessica explained. "Kaden told us that he was going to play T-ball, so I figured you would be at the sign-ups on Saturday. I thought Kaden could ride home with us and you could pick him up that evening if that's okay. I'm sure the boys would love to spend more time together. And Lainey could play with them, too."

That was actually a good idea, because it'd give Kaden a chance to play with an older child and a younger one, too. Mandy had read in one of her parenting books that it was important for a child to be able to adapt to playing with children of all ages, not simply their own peers. Plus, she was certain Kaden would like that, particularly a chance to feel like the "big boy," as well.

"Can I, Aunt Mandy? Please?"

She nodded. "Sure you can."

"We can practice hitting and catching and stuff," Nathan said to Kaden. "Last year I was on the Cardinals and Dad was coach, so he's gonna try to get Cardinals again since we already bought all the matching batting helmets and stuff."

"Will I be on the Cardinals?" Kaden asked.

"You have to wait and see. You'll be doing T-ball, right? I did T-ball last year, but this year, I'm on coach pitch. That means my Dad will be throwing the ball at me."

Jessica laughed. "He'll be throwing it *to* you, hopefully not *at* you."

Nathan grinned. "Yeah, that's what I meant."

Mandy noticed Kaden flinch when Nathan mentioned his dad, and it broke her heart. "You will like T-ball, Kaden," she said, trying her best to sound encouraging.

Kaden's blue eyes grew wide. "I'm gonna hit the ball and run fast."

Nathan laughed. "Yep, I know. That's the way not to get out."

Kaden nodded, but Mandy could see the confusion playing across his face. He wasn't sure about all of the ins and outs of the game, other than what she'd attempted to teach him by watching the Braves on TV. "I don't want to get out," Kaden said, obviously remembering that that wasn't a good thing.

"That's right," Nathan said, his green eyes growing wide, too. "You don't."

"Maybe your Aunt Mandy and I can take you to the field to practice before the sign-ups on Saturday," Daniel offered, then looked to Mandy.

She was floored. Daniel was opening the

door for her to be included in his one-on-one time, and she had to admit she was thrilled.

"What do you think, Mandy? Want to do that one afternoon?" Daniel asked.

"Yes, that's fine," she answered, curbing the enthusiasm in her tone. Truthfully, it was way more than fine. It was perfect, not only because she'd get to see Kaden during Daniel's time but also because she wasn't all that great at sports growing up, and time really hadn't changed that. Having a guy around to show Kaden the ropes could come in handy, even if that guy was Daniel.

"So we'll see you at the sign-ups Saturday morning," Jessica said. "Now, let's go, Nathan. I need to go get supper started before your dad gets home from the college."

"Chad still teaching at Stockville?" Daniel asked.

"Yes," Jessica said. "Advanced Biology. Oh, that reminds me, he wants to talk to you about a support group that has started on campus that he thought you might be interested in. It's for people who have lost—" she glanced at Kaden and saw that he and Nathan were engrossed in a chat about team colors "—people who have lost loved ones to drunk driving accidents," she added at a whisper.

Daniel nodded thoughtfully. "I would definitely be interested."

Jessica looked to Mandy. "And Mandy, if you change your mind, I think it'd be good for you, too."

"Thanks, but I don't think so."

Jessica nodded, and though Mandy didn't look at him, she knew Daniel surveyed her every emotion. She kept her face placid and her attention on the boys.

"Come on, Nathan," Jessica coaxed, and they worked their way down the hallway and through the gallery to the front door with Daniel, Mandy and Kaden following behind.

"Hey, look, there's John." Jessica pointed outside where John Cutter stood near the front door looking at the photos in the display window. She said a few words to John as she left, and John took advantage of the opened door to enter the gallery.

"Hey, Mandy," he said, removing a faded denim cap and stuffing it in his back pocket. "I wasn't sure if your shop was still open and didn't want to barge in if you were closed."

"If we're home, we're open for business," Kaden said, "unless we're eating or sleeping."

"Well, next time, I'll know." Then John looked past Mandy to Daniel and grinned broadly. "Hey, I heard you were coming back. Sure will be great to have you on the team again. Got a shortstop position wide open for ya, you know."

Daniel nodded. "I believe that can be arranged."

"Good deal," John said.

"So do you need some pictures taken, John?" Mandy asked. John Cutter was older than Mandy. In fact, he'd been in the same grade as Mia, Jacob and Daniel in school so she knew him from the baseball team. John had also been a church regular growing up, so whenever she did go to church, she'd seen him there. But they weren't overly close, so she could only assume he was here for photos.

"Yeah," he said. "Well, not for me, but for Casey. He's graduating this year and I kind of forgot about the whole graduation picture thing until the school sent home a letter for me to place his order for invitations." He frowned. "I wasn't all that certain he'd be graduating for a while, but according to Principal Lawson, he's turned his grades around this spring." John grinned. "I was surprised about that, but in a good way. Got a feeling it has something to do with a girl he's trying to impress."

"I can see that happening." Daniel chuckled.

"Yeah, well, he's had a rough time of things ever since Mom—well, you know, he's raised by me now, and I'm working three jobs, so I can't be around to help with homework. I can't blame him for having a rough spot with the grades for a while, but I am glad he's turned things around, though."

"I'm glad, too," Mandy said. She now remembered the history of the Cutter family. The family had a large farm about halfway between Claremont and Stockville, and John's father had died in a farming accident when John was in high school and Casey was in elementary school. Unable to cope with her husband's death, their mother turned to painkillers to deal with her grief and had ended up overdosing a few years later. John had been left to raise Casey.

"The thing is, I asked him to come over here today and see you, make an appointment for pictures or whatever. I thought maybe you could take some out at the farm."

"I can do that," Mandy said. "Just let me know when."

John nodded, but Mandy could tell he was bothered. "So you haven't seen Casey today?" he asked.

"No, but I was gone for a while to take some photos at Hydrangea Park. Maybe he came by then," Mandy said.

"Yeah, maybe." John glanced out the front door, where the tiny white lights that illuminated the buildings on the town square at night were tossing a pretty golden glow over the darkness and causing the three-tiered fountain in the center of the square to sparkle. "I guess he didn't get a chance to come by," John said, then looked to Daniel. "You're working with the youth at the church now, right?"

"I am. Is Casey in the teen group? I'm teaching that class tomorrow night, you know, so maybe I'll see him. Hard to believe he's a senior."

"Hopefully you'll see him," John said. "See, I'm working second shift now at the steel mill, so I haven't been able to go to church on Wednesdays, and he typically doesn't go as much if I'm not nudging him."

Daniel nodded. "That happens with a lot of teens, but I'm hoping to strengthen the youth program enough that they'll actually want to come. I've already selected what I hope is a teen-worthy curriculum and have several bonding activities planned for the rest of the spring and summer months."

"That's good," John said. "And he may show back up on his own now, anyway. The girl I believe he likes is a church girl." He grinned. "Gotta admit, I kind of prayed for that. Figured it'd take some kind of outside interest to really get him back to church after we lost Mom. Think God answered my prayers in the form of Nadia Berry."

"Brother Henry's granddaughter?" Mandy asked.

"Yes, that's her," John said.

"She came by the gallery yesterday and asked if I was interested in hiring anyone for the afternoon hours, said she was putting in applications around the square so she could save up and buy a car." Mandy recalled the pretty girl and her sweet disposition. "I've been thinking about it through the day today and was planning to give her a call later. I could probably use someone here to answer questions, help customers and all while I'm doing shoots away from the studio."

"Well, from what I know of Nadia, she'd be terrific for that," John said. "She's a good kid and comes from a great family. Like I said, I believe she may be the answer to my prayers, as far as Casey is concerned. Anyway, I just wanted to see if he'd come by because I got off work early and couldn't find him."

"I'm sorry," Mandy said. "I haven't seen him or heard from him."

John nodded. "Can't get an answer on his cell, either, but he's not great about answering. I'm sure he's fine. Well, I hope he's fine. He's been spending a lot of time with a rough crowd, and I've been a little worried. I thought the fact that he was trying to impress Nadia might be enough to keep him away from that group, but you know teens. Peer pressure and all."

He grabbed the baseball cap out of his pocket and pushed it low on his head. Mandy thought he'd say more about Casey, but he seemed to think better of it and sighed. "Mandy, I'll make sure he comes by and makes that appointment soon. We're running behind on the pictures."

"Sounds good," she said, smiling. "I'm pretty fast about getting them developed and ready, so once we take the photos, we'll be good to go. No worries," she said, feeling a tug at her heart for everything John was going through, working three jobs and raising a teen. Someday she'd be raising a teen, too. The little sandy haired blond currently getting bored with the adult conversation and performing one of his favorite pastimes of weaving in and out of the gallery easels while making race car noises.

"Thanks, Mandy," John said. "I appreciate it. And Daniel, if you could let me know how you think he's doing, you know, with his faith and all, I'd sure appreciate that, too. I do my best, but it's hard when I'm working all the time."

"You can count on it," Daniel said.

John nodded, said his goodbyes and left.

With arms in front of him holding an imaginary steering wheel, Kaden made a screeching brakes noise as he neared the door and asked, "Are we closed for business now?"

"Yes, we are. It's about time for dinner," Mandy said.

Kaden reached for the sign and flipped it over. "Taco soup, right?"

"That's right," she said, feeling a little awkward having a normal nightly conversation with Kaden while Daniel stood nearby. Families did things like this, talked about their day and what they'd have for dinner and then hung around together visiting at night. It reminded her vaguely of growing up, her and Mia with their grandparents. That was the only family she'd ever known, and even though they weren't a conventional family, they were a family just the same. So she knew what family, real family, felt like. And she missed it.

"Uncle Daniel said he hoped he can stay to eat," Kaden announced.

Daniel cleared his throat. "Well, I said the soup smelled good."

"And you said you hoped to eat some with us," Kaden said, his blue eyes wide as though daring Daniel to disagree.

"That's one of the things I've learned about having a four-year-old around," Mandy said.

"What's that?" Daniel asked, his face a little flushed from getting caught inviting himself to dinner.

"If you don't want something repeated, you'd better just keep it to yourself."

He held up a finger. "Duly noted."

She walked beside him as they followed Kaden back toward the kitchen and was once again reminded of the difference in having a male in the gallery. The hallway was plenty big enough for Mandy and Kaden to walk side by side, but with Daniel beside her, the space was filled. Consequently she found herself brushing against him, his arm's occasional contact with hers sending a tremor of awareness through her senses. Mandy attempted to edge closer to her side of the wall and was discomforted to find herself both happy and sad when the hallway ended and she stepped away from the impressive man.

Deep down, she really didn't want him to leave yet. Mandy didn't want to spend a whole lot of time analyzing why not. The truth was, he'd said he wanted to stay for dinner, and she would've asked him no matter who he was. Southern hospitality was something she could handle. Her attraction to a man who wanted to take Kaden away wasn't. But she'd work on that day-by-day, somehow.

"You can stay for dinner if you want. I'm guessing that you didn't get taco soup all that often in Africa."

He laughed, and the sound sent another happy tremor along her spine. "Not once."

"So you're staying?" Kaden asked.

"Yes, I'm staying," Daniel answered, while Mandy began grabbing things out of the fridge and then getting the bowls from the counter. Those were the same words he'd said earlier, and naturally they reminded her of the other words he'd repeated.

"I want custody."

She'd said the same words, but unfortunately, hers sounded more like a plea. His was a proclamation.

Chapter Five

Daniel sat at the table with a steaming bowl of taco soup teasing his nostrils. A bag of tortilla chips, a bowl of shredded cheese and another bowl of sour cream centered the table. Tall glasses of iced sweet tea stood by Daniel's and Mandy's bowls, and a short glass of milk completed Kaden's place setting.

Mandy hadn't looked Daniel in the eye since he'd mentioned custody, but he could tell she hadn't stopped thinking about it. The worry on her face was evident. He didn't like upsetting her, but his mind was made up. Why didn't she see that this was a good thing? He'd come back to let her have the life she wanted, see the world the way she wanted. That should have made her happy, right?

She didn't look happy. She looked as if she

really meant it when she said she wanted to keep custody. But he knew Mandy, and she'd wanted to get away from this small town for as long as he remembered. Everything about Mandy screamed big city. She was runway model beautiful, with a talent that matched her beauty and a desire to follow that talent wherever it led. He had to commend her for her willingness to give up the dream and stay in Claremont. But he didn't believe that sacrifice would last forever.

"You're gonna love the soup," Kaden said. "It's my favorite." He crooked his mouth to the side. "Except, so is spaghetti and meatballs. And sometimes steak. And I like macaroni, but only if it's the really cheesy one. That's the kind Aunt Mandy makes."

Daniel grinned. "Well, this looks amazing."

"It is," Kaden said.

"Thanks," Mandy said softly.

Daniel had been surprised by what he'd already seen in Mandy and Kaden's home, all of the evidence of her attempts to be a good parent. And by all indications, she was accomplishing that goal. Kaden seemed happy, even if the sadness of losing his parents did work its way subtly into his life. His state-

ment about Daniel and Jacob's old red truck
had punched Daniel in the gut. He should
have remembered that Jacob drove that truck.
But that was okay. He didn't want Kaden to
forget his parents. On the contrary, he wanted
him to remember how much they loved him,
and obviously Kaden had good memories
about himself with Jacob in that old truck.

Daniel thought of the photos in Kaden's
room and knew that Mandy wanted the
same thing. In fact, though he was certain she didn't know it, his admiration for
Mandy Carter had skyrocketed in the past
few hours. She wasn't the same person she'd
been in high school, and he suspected he had
only scratched the surface of the real woman
behind the tough-girl facade.

But he wasn't completely certain that her
itch to leave wouldn't get the best of her eventually. And she did need help, not only whenever Kaden was sick. She needed help feeling
content again. In truth, Mandy Carter needed
more than Daniel. She needed God.

"Mind if I say grace before we start?" he
asked, holding out a hand toward each of
them.

Kaden frowned. "You can if you want,
I guess."

"He really likes to say the blessing," Mandy explained. "And he's very good at it."

Daniel's surprise must have shown on his face, because Mandy lifted a dark brow and asked, "Is that okay with you, for Kaden to say grace the way he always does?"

Feeling guilty for his presumption, Daniel grinned. "Yes, of course. That's fine."

"And then after dinner you can go up and help him say his prayers," she said. "The way he always does before bed."

Daniel mouthed, "I'm sorry."

And Mandy, being Mandy, mouthed, "I know."

Daniel's laugh rolled out, and Kaden, who'd already bowed his head, jerked his eyes open. "You okay, Uncle Daniel?"

"Yes," he said. "Yes, I'm fine. Please say the blessing so we can eat this delicious meal."

"Okay." He bowed his head and began a tender rendition of God is great, God is good that touched Daniel's heart. Then immediately following the amen, Kaden chimed, "Dig in!" and Daniel was treated to one of the best meals he'd had in months.

Yes, the food was good—the seasoned taco meat, tomato sauce, corn and chili beans delighting his taste buds—but the meal's appeal was much more than that. It was the chatter between bites, with Kaden talking all about his new friend Nathan and the Little League team that he'd be on after Saturday's sign-ups and the kinds of animals that he'd bought at the craft store for his wilderness lodge. And it was a time of watching Mandy drinking in every word their nephew said and smiling as though there were nothing more important than this meal and this conversation with Kaden.

After they finished eating, Daniel started to help Mandy clear the table, but she shooed him away. "No, you've been gone awhile and would probably like to do story time tonight." She looked at Kaden. "Okay with you for Uncle Daniel to read you a story and help you say prayers while I clean up the kitchen?"

"Sure," Kaden said, then took Daniel's hand. "Come on."

"Okay," he answered then to Mandy said, "Thanks."

She never looked up from putting the dishes in the sink. "You're welcome."

They reached Kaden's room, and the four-year-old immediately went to the second drawer in his nightstand and rummaged through the clothes until he withdrew a pair of pajamas covered in red, gold and blue Tonka trucks.

"I put my pj's on first, then I have to brush my teeth, and then we read a story."

"Got it," Daniel said, impressed with the ritual. He wondered if it'd been started by Mia and Jacob, or by Mandy herself. In either case Kaden had a routine and was comfortable with it, and Daniel couldn't have been more pleased. He watched as Kaden entered the bathroom and listened to the water running and the gentle scrubbing of his toothbrush against his teeth. The entire scenario was absolutely precious, a little boy growing up right before his eyes. And right before Mandy's eyes, for the past nine months.

After a few minutes Kaden returned with the slight scent of mint toothpaste accompanying him as he returned. "How'd I do?" He smiled broadly, and two rows of tiny baby teeth filled his grin. Then he opened his mouth wide so Daniel could check the back ones, too.

"They look good to me," Daniel said.

Kaden nodded as though this was the correct answer.

Bemused, Daniel asked, "Okay, so now we read?"

"Yep." Already on his knees in front of the bookshelf, Kaden thumbed through the books. "I'm looking for my favorite."

"Do you need help finding it?"

"Nope, here it is." Kaden withdrew a thin book and brought it to Daniel, who sat on the bed.

Kaden pulled back the covers and climbed inside. "Aunt Mandy climbs in with me," he said, holding the covers back for Daniel.

Daniel slipped his shoes off. "Okay." Then he snuggled in beside his nephew. A glimpse of a memory played through his head…Jacob describing the wonderment of parenthood and how amazing the smallest things were when you shared them with your child. He'd specifically described the tenderness of tucking Kaden in at night. Now Daniel would also know how that felt. He swallowed, missing his brother terribly and hating it that Kaden would no longer have this kind of moment with Jacob.

"You in?" Kaden asked, peering toward the edge of the bed as though expecting to see Daniel's feet hanging out.

"I'm in," he said with a grin.

"Cool." Kaden leaned against the pillow.

"You read it, but I need to see the pictures while you do." He pointed to the book.

Daniel had been so absorbed in reminiscing about Jacob's words that he'd forgotten the main reason they were here. He nodded, looked down at the cover of the book, and read *The Story of Moses.*

He'd noticed the Bible story books on the shelves earlier, but he was a bit surprised that this one was Kaden's favorite.

"I know the first two pages," Kaden said. "Aunt Mandy lets me read those."

"Then I will, too," Daniel said, opening the book to the first page, which showed baby Moses in a basket floating in the river.

"Moses needed someone special to take care of him, because his mommy couldn't. She wanted to find the perfect person to take care of him." The words weren't exactly what was on the page, but were fairly close. "That's his sister, watching to make sure that the princess finds him," Kaden added, pointing to Moses' sister, Miriam, peeking through the bulrushes.

"Very good," Daniel said, and turned the page.

"The princess took Moses into the castle and was like his mommy for while he grew up, and Moses was happy that the princess was taking care of him." Kaden looked up. "Right?"

Daniel nodded. "Yes, that's right. You're doing a great job," he said, turning the page.

"Now you read," Kaden said. "I haven't learned the other pages yet.

"Okay." Daniel continued with the remainder of the story, how Moses led his people from the land of Egypt and how he became a friend of God and brought God's people the Ten Commandments. When he finished the story, Kaden shimmied down farther into the covers.

"I say my prayers now," he said.

"I see. Do you want to say yours first, or do you want me to say mine first?"

Kaden's mouth opened. "You're saying prayers, too?"

And then Daniel saw the hole in this scenario. Mandy was keeping Kaden aware of God's presence, but she wasn't joining in to trust Him on her own. "Yes, I'm definitely saying prayers, too."

"Okay," Kaden said with a smile. "Then you first."

Daniel bowed his head. "Dear Heavenly Father, thank you so much for bringing me home safely and letting me get back to see Mandy and Kaden again. Thank you for my new job at the church, and thank you for taking such good care of Mandy and Kaden while I was away. Help us to always put You first and to remember that with You by our side there is nothing we can't do. We love You, God. In Your Son's precious name, amen." He opened his eyes to see Kaden peering up at him.

"That was a good one, Uncle Daniel."

Daniel smiled. "Thanks. Now your turn."

Kaden nodded, bowed his sandy waves. "Now I lay me down to sleep. I pray the Lord my soul to keep. If I should die before I wake, I pray the Lord my soul to take. God bless Aunt Mandy and Uncle Daniel and Nathan and Nathan's mommy and Lainey. And God, please let me get on a fun team on Saturday and let me learn how to not get out. And God, thank you for bringing Uncle Daniel home. And God, please tell Mommy and Daddy that I love them as big as the sky. In Jesus' name, amen."

Daniel swallowed, unable to speak for a moment, then he said, "Kaden, *that* was a good one."

"Thanks." He plopped his head against the

pillow, then looked at Daniel. "Aunt Mandy fluffs my pillow and then gives me a good-night kiss."

"Got it," Daniel said, reaching behind Kaden's head to squeeze the pillow.

Kaden laughed. "Not like that." He lifted his head, squirmed around until he was on his knees, balled his fists and began punching the sides of the pillow. "She does it like this, but harder. She says sometimes it makes her happy to do it this way."

Daniel bit his lip to keep from laughing. He suspected that she'd occasionally punched that pillow while picturing it was Daniel's head. "All right," he said, and punched right along with Kaden.

"Yep, that's it," Kaden said, when the pillow had been punched and pummeled to death. "Now it's ready." He bounced around and let his head sink in the middle of the properly fluffed rectangle.

"Alright, then," Daniel said, easing off the bed and then bringing the comforter up to Kaden's neck and kissing his forehead. "Sweet dreams."

"Hey, that's what Aunt Mandy says," Kaden said, smiling broadly. "Good job."

"Thanks." Daniel headed to the kitchen, where Mandy was wiping down the table.

"Everything go okay?" she asked, holding her hand along the edge and guiding the tortilla chip crumbs into her palm.

"Yes, fine."

She moved to the sink, tossed the dish cloth in one side and then crossed the kitchen to dust her palms over the trash can. "I knew he'd enjoy having you read to him."

"And saying prayers with him," Daniel said, wondering if she'd mention that Kaden typically is the only one saying prayers.

She didn't.

"That's great." She washed her hands, dried them off with a towel. Then she turned and leaned against the counter. "I think that it's a good idea for you to help Kaden learn a little about baseball before Saturday. I've tried to show him the game by watching the Braves whenever I know they're on, but I'm thinking television probably isn't nearly as good as actually getting on a field."

"Well, it didn't hurt, I'm sure. But practicing on a real field will be good for him, too. Tomorrow would be kind of tough for me to pull off, since I've got the teen class lesson to prepare before church tomorrow night." He looked over at her. "The teens are a good group, according to Brother Henry, but they're dealing with typical teen issues— and he's hoping I can help them with that."

She nodded. "Maybe you'll be able to help John Cutter's little brother."

"I plan to try."

"You know, you were talking about Kaden going to your place after church tomorrow night, but what are you going to do with him during the day on Thursday and Friday when you're working at the church?"

"I planned to take him along. There's a playground at the church, and we could bring some of his toys and things." Daniel had assumed Kaden would simply tag along with him to his church activities, but her question did have him wondering whether he could get his work done and entertain a four-year-old throughout the day.

"That would probably be okay," she said, twisting the towel between her hands as she spoke. "He still naps most days, so you might want to bring a pillow and blanket along to the church."

"He still naps?" Daniel asked.

She smiled, a beautiful expression that lit up her entire face. "Actually, the kids in kindergarten still nap, too. I think they stop that at the school in first grade, but Kaden still gets really cranky if he doesn't get a nap. Trust me, you don't want to see it."

"Then I will definitely add a nap to the daily schedule," Daniel said wryly. That would help Daniel, as well, since he could probably get a good deal of work done during Kaden's nap. He was fairly certain there was a portable cot in the attic at his parents' house. He could set Kaden up with a nap spot in his church office.

"He'll only sleep in the daytime if he has his nighty-night," she said. "It's the blanket your mother made for him when he was born. He likes to rub the satin corner between his fingers when he goes to sleep. He doesn't need it at night, but he likes to have it during the day." She paused then added, "That started after Jacob and Mia died."

"Will you make sure to pack that with his things tomorrow?"

"Yes, but I wanted to make sure you knew to bring it with you to the church if he's going to take his naps there."

Daniel was beginning to realize that he had a lot to learn about a four-year-old's daily schedule. He appreciated Mandy showing him the ropes. "Thanks."

She sighed. "I just want him to be happy, you know." Then she turned dark eyes up to Daniel. "I love him, and I believe I'm good for him, Daniel."

Daniel took a small step closer to her, close enough that he could see the worry and concern for Kaden in her eyes. Amazingly, Mandy was even prettier when she lowered her guard and gave him a glimpse of her heart. "I love him, too, Mandy. And I don't doubt that you do. But let's give this a try. Let him spend a few days with me and see how it goes." He exhaled slowly. "Then we'll discuss the whole custody thing again. I don't want to fight with you. I only want what's best for Kaden."

"That's what I want, too."

"Okay," he said, smiling. "We agree on that." He recalled the words Bo Taylor said to him earlier and repeated them now. "A child needs that—people who care and are working together for his or her best interest. Family." Daniel didn't add Bo's last part, "People who love each other," but he prayed that if they both loved Kaden, the sense of family would still be evident in his nephew's world.

"Kaden does need family," she whispered, her brows now drawn together as she pondered Daniel's words.

"After he has spent a little time with me, we can reassess what's best. And in the meantime, we can try to get along and stop debating the custody issue."

"Kind of hard not to think about it," she said.

"I didn't say we wouldn't think about it. We just won't debate it until I have a little time with Kaden and see how he adjusts to me as a parent figure. Deal?"

She tilted her head, gave a reluctant nod. "I guess it has to be."

"Okay, then I'll plan to pick him up tomorrow before church, say six o'clock?"

She nodded. "I'll have his things ready."

"You could come to church, too, you know."

"I don't think so."

Daniel didn't press the issue, but he wasn't giving up on restoring Mandy's faith yet.

"And we can all go to the Little League field together Thursday afternoon if you want. Kaden and I will come pick you up after I finish up at the church that afternoon."

"That sounds good," she said. "But he needs a bat and a glove. Well, he needs everything, and I haven't exactly known what to buy or where to buy it. I was kind of waiting for the sign-ups and hoping they would tell me what to purchase."

Daniel had an idea about obtaining a few of the things Kaden would need, but he'd have to do a little investigating in his parents' attic before he would know for certain. He decided he'd do a thorough search when he went to find the old cot.

"We'll start out at Mr. Bowers's Sporting Goods Thursday afternoon to get what he needs. Then we'll head on over to the field." Daniel could visibly see the relief spread across her face.

"That would be great," she said. "I didn't even know what size glove to get or what kind of bat. There are different kinds, right?"

"Right," he said with a grin. "But I can help with all of that."

Mandy closed her eyes and kept them that way for a moment. Then she opened them and said, "Okay. Thanks, Daniel."

He wasn't sure exactly what she was thanking him for, but he said, "You're welcome."

They stood in the small rear entry that separated the kitchen from the back door. The room wasn't lit beyond the kitchen light casting them in shadow, and Mandy's petite silhouette made her look tiny and fragile. Daniel had the sudden urge to take her in his arms and embrace her, assure her that everything would be okay and that she would never lose Kaden completely even if Daniel did gain custody. But Mandy was proud of her independence, and he didn't think she'd take kindly to the guy trying to get custody of Kaden giving her a shoulder to cry on.

No matter how much he wanted to hold her right now.

Chapter Six

There were forty kids on the roster for the teen class at Claremont Community Church, but only six girls made a showing when it was time for class to begin Wednesday night. Daniel couldn't tell whether they were overly happy to be here, but each of their faces clearly held curiosity when they walked in and found him sitting on the desk with a huge photo of the Serengeti mounted on the wall at the front of the room.

"Wow, what's that?" a tall, blue-eyed blonde asked. Sitting with two of her friends, she pointed to the colorful photo that Daniel had taken earlier this year.

He followed her finger and answered, "That's a wildebeest."

"Wow, cool," she said, her voice leaning toward flirtatious. "It looks dangerous.

Like you were really close to it. Did you take the picture?"

"I did," Daniel answered.

The girls sat in two groups of three, and Daniel easily categorized the clusters as the pretty, leggy cheerleaders and the quiet, shy wallflowers.

"You may not remember us, but we met you last year when you did the slideshow," the chatty blonde continued. "We were *so* excited to hear you would be teaching our class. I'm RileyAnn Marker, and this is Theapia Best and Jasmine Waddell." Theapia, a striking, tall black girl, gave Daniel a wave of pink-tipped fingers and Jasmine, a shorter image of RileyAnn with blue eyes and silky blond hair, emitted a bubbly, "Hey."

"So, do we call you Mr. Brantley, or can we call you Daniel?" Theapia asked.

"Mr. Brantley," Daniel said in his best assertive voice. He hoped it wouldn't take RileyAnn and her cohorts long to realize that he was their teacher and more than a decade older than all of them. He'd always heard it was best for a youth minister to be married, even if not required by the job description. This, he supposed, was one of the main reasons. Flirty teenagers. He turned his attention to the other trio of girls in the room. "And what are your names?"

"Aaliyah Smith," a willowy blonde answered. She had the look of the three cheerleaders but lacked the confidence. Her words were barely spoken and she avoided eye contact when she continued, "I just moved to Claremont last fall, so I didn't see your slideshow. But I heard it was really good."

"I'll bring in plenty of photos and Power-Point presentations about the church's missions in Africa, so you don't have to worry that you missed it. But this class isn't going to be focused on my Africa trips. We can talk about them some and explore any mission work that all of you may want to try in the future, but we'll primarily cover the types of things you deal with day-to-day." He cleared his throat. "It hasn't been that long since I was a teen, so I remember everything you go through. Peer pressure, teen temptations, basically finding your place in the adult world."

Wanting to keep the atmosphere light and the conversation topics open, Daniel edged down from the desk and propped against the side to lean toward the kids. Clasping his fingers, he said, "Things tend to be a little more difficult when you're a teen, if my memory serves. Like moving to a new city and starting a new high school. I'm sure that wasn't easy, huh?" he asked Aaliyah.

"No," she answered, and this time her voice was a little more compelling, and she looked directly at Daniel. "It wasn't."

He nodded. "We'll talk about that, because you realize that what you went through last year is something that a lot of your classmates here will go through soon, moving and starting over."

Theapia shifted in her seat. "How's that?" she asked, her brows raised in question. "Who's moving?"

"Well, how old are you?" Daniel asked.

"Sixteen."

"You're what, a sophomore?"

"A junior," Theapia said. "I'm seventeen next month."

"Okay, then next year you'll graduate. Are you planning to go to college?"

"Either Georgia Tech or Auburn." Her bright smile conveyed her enthusiasm for the next stage in life.

"And to attend either of those schools, you'll move away, won't you? Start over in a new town, make new friends, the way Aaliyah did this year."

Aaliyah looked up and caught Theapia's gaze.

"Maybe Aaliyah can help those of you who are moving next year by letting you know how she adjusted to life here this year," Daniel said.

Aaliyah shrugged shyly. "I'm not that sure I've adjusted that well."

"Then maybe some of your friends in this class can help you with that, and perhaps that type of favor will be reciprocated to them when they get to college."

One of Theapia's dark brows lifted and she nodded slightly. "Yeah, okay. I can see that."

Daniel could tell he was making headway, because all of the girls were paying attention now. He said a silent thanks to God for helping him find a way to break through their communication barriers. *Stay with me, Lord.* "A lot of times in life you're going to be placed in situations you didn't plan on, put in locations that are unfamiliar and surrounded by people you may not know. What I'd like to do in this class is prepare you for those times and help you form something of a support group with each other right here in Claremont."

"A support group?" Aaliyah asked.

Daniel smiled. "Thanks to Facebook, Twitter and other social networks yet to come, you can always stay in touch and encourage each other along the way. I know I made a lot of new friends during my mission trips—" he pointed to some smaller photos on the side wall of the church groups he started in Tanzania and Malawi "—but I also stayed close and relied on my friends from Claremont to pull me through when times got tough, or when I was a little scared about the future."

An image of Mandy flashed in his mind, the look on her face when he picked up Kaden tonight and put his small suitcase in the truck. She was scared about her future, about possibly losing custody of Kaden, and Daniel wanted to do what he could to reassure her. No matter whether he had custody of Kaden or not, she would always have a place in Kaden's life. Always.

"Were you scared when you took the picture?" a redhead sitting beside Aaliyah asked. "Of that animal, I mean?"

"The wildebeest?" Daniel asked.

She nodded, sending red spirals bouncing against freckled shoulders.

"Nah, as long as I didn't bother him, he wasn't interested in bothering me," Daniel said. Remembering that name recognition was important, especially to teens who were already struggling with finding their identity in the world, Daniel asked, "What's your name?"

She smiled. "Catherine. Catherine Blaire."

"Nice to meet you, Catherine," Daniel said, then smiled at the only girl remaining. "And how about you? What's your name?"

Her inky black hair was shiny, long and straight, and when she looked at Daniel he noticed Asian features, unique eyes and beautiful light caramel skin. "I'm Nadia Berry," she answered with a bright smile. She was soft-spoken but still had an edge of confidence to her tone. Daniel recalled John Cutter's words last night about his little brother and that Nadia Berry had captured Casey's interest. Daniel could see that happening with the pretty girl. She nodded toward the photo behind Daniel. "You said we'll talk about mission work in this class?"

"Yes, are you interested in missions?" Daniel asked.

"I am. I'd like to visit Africa one day, but I would also like to visit Thailand. My parents adopted me from Thailand, so naturally I'm interested in my heritage and in bringing Christ to people there."

Daniel nodded. No wonder she'd captured Casey's attention. She was not only pretty, but she was Godly and intelligent, as well. "I've actually already talked to Brother Henry— your grandfather—about taking the teens on a mission trip over the Christmas holiday this year. We're tossing around a few ideas. Right now it looks as though we will visit Trinidad, but I'll ask him about a trip to Thailand in the future."

"I've asked him, too, and he said that we may be able to go one day," she said, still smiling. "I'd like to go on the Trinidad trip also."

"I'd like that, too," Jasmine said, grinning at Nadia. Nadia returned the smile, and Daniel was pleased that already the two groups of girls seemed to be merging on one of his topics.

After a few more minutes of chatting about potential mission trips, the door opened and three boys noisily entered the room. Two of them looked around fourteen or fifteen, still in that awkward stage of half boy, half man and attempting to impress the other older boy that walked in behind them. The first two kids settled into seats between the two pods of girls and offered a couple of lackadaisical Sorry-we're-late remarks toward Daniel.

The older one took his time entering the classroom, nodded toward Daniel and then grinned at the giggling girls before slumping into the center chair. Even though his hair was long and shaggy, and his white T-shirt and jeans put him in a John Travolta *Grease* manifestation, Daniel had no trouble recognizing the strong jaw line, broad shoulders and athletic build of a Cutter. He looked just like John, but younger. A thick wave of light brown hair covered one eye completely, and he slung it to the side when he sat down, but it quickly fell back into place over the hiding eye.

The cheerleader group giggled, Aaliyah and Catherine blushed, and Nadia turned her attention to her opened Bible. Daniel noticed John's brother angling in his seat so that he could catch a glimpse of the pretty Asian girl, but Nadia didn't look up from the verses she was suddenly studying with keen interest.

"And your names?" Daniel asked the boys,

deciding not to lecture them on tardiness during his first go at the class.

"Aaron Shields," the youngest boy answered.

"Cory Shields," the other said. "We're cousins."

Everyone waited for John's brother to follow suit, but he merely picked up a pencil and began twirling it through his fingers while Theapia, RileyAnn and Jasmine smothered their giggles.

"And you're Casey Cutter," Daniel said, causing the boy to do another hair flip and then glance up questioningly at his new teacher.

"You know me?" he asked.

"I played baseball with your brother in high school," Daniel said. "He's still a good friend."

"Yeah, well, he's working tonight." Casey turned the pencil a few more times and then changed from twirling it to thumping it against the top of his desk. "He works all the time now."

"That's what he said. Well, I'm glad you made it to church tonight."

The boy flipped the brown waves again and shot another glance toward Nadia. Then his mouth flattened and his shoulders slumped slightly. "Yeah, well, I didn't have anything else to do."

Like Daniel had told the class earlier, it hadn't been that long since he'd been a teenager, and he knew the look of a boy attempting to act like he was tough and apathetic. He also knew that most of the teens that fell into that category were actually the ones hurting the most, needing the most. Casey Cutter was going to be a challenge, but Daniel was up for the test.

He used the remainder of the class time to gauge the kids, learn their interests and see what topics might be most appealing for Wednesday night Bible studies. He wanted Wednesdays to be more active, more fun and less sedentary, and the kids seemed to appreciate that goal. By the end of the class, they'd all voted to start a video study on Wednesdays where they would watch an episode of *The Andy Griffith Show* and then discuss the moral lesson to the show.

"Andy Griffith is full of Biblical principles," Daniel had told Brother Henry earlier today. "And the Mayberry lessons will give teens the chance to have something of a movie night in their midweek study and break away from feeling like they're getting another hour of school at night. Might even get more teens to come to the midweek study."

Brother Henry had agreed, and from all indications, the idea seemed to be a good one. Several of the kids were already talking about inviting friends to next week's study, bringing popcorn and making it a fun fellowship.

Daniel ended the class feeling he had reached his goal with starting off on the right foot, even if Casey Cutter had seemed the least impressed of the bunch.

As the kids left, several of the girls told Daniel they'd enjoyed the lesson, the younger boys told him they'd see him Sunday, and Casey lagged behind while Nadia organized her notes and her Bible.

"So, you going to the baseball game Friday night?" Casey asked her as she slid the items into her church tote.

"I don't think so," she said. "My grandfather has invited all of the family over for a fish fry Friday night."

"Oh, well, we have a home game Friday," Casey said.

"The team's doing pretty good, isn't it? I haven't got to go to a game yet, but I heard them announce it on the closed circuit TV at school." She settled her tote strap on her shoulder. "I think they said you got a home run last time, didn't you?"

Casey's shoulders seemed to broaden as he shrugged and smiled. "I, uh, yeah. I actually got two."

"That's great," she said and gave him a full grin.

"Well, maybe you can come see my team play sometime."

"I'll try," she said.

"Yeah, well, that sounds good." He turned and started his tough-guy walk toward the door, but slowed when Nadia cleared her throat.

"Casey?" she asked.

He stopped on a dime, turned and flipped his hair out of his eye while Daniel attempted to look busy gathering the books at his desk. "Yeah?" Casey answered.

"When is your next home game? I mean, after this Friday's game."

A glimmer of hope surfaced on Casey's face. "A week from Saturday."

"I think I can come to that one."

Casey's smile tossed the tough-guy facade right out the window and gave Daniel no doubt that he really liked this girl. "If you do, maybe I could, like, take you home after, if you need a ride or anything like that," he said.

The blush on her cheeks was instant. "That sounds good."

Casey did a pretty good job hiding his excitement, even if Daniel could tell the kid wanted to shout for joy. Instead, he motioned toward the hall.

"You want to walk with me to the auditorium?"

"Sure."

The pair left the classroom, while Daniel continued busying himself with pretty much nothing around his desk until they were gone. Then he closed his eyes and silently prayed, *Lord, let Casey learn that he doesn't need to hide behind that tough-guy veneer. And let me help him to overcome the pain of losing his parents. Help me bring him back to You, God. And help Nadia do the same thing, Lord. I think you're using her to help that young man, and I think it's wonderful. Use me, too, God. Let me do Your will with Casey and with all of the young lives that I might touch at Claremont.*

Daniel thought of another life he had an opportunity to change and to touch. *And Lord, let me do Your will with Mandy, too. Help me to say the right thing, do the right thing, when it comes to custody of Kaden. And if it be Your will, Lord, help me bring her back to You.*

Brother Henry knocked and stepped into the classroom. "Hey Daniel, I just saw Kaden heading from class toward the auditorium for the closing announcements. I wanted to ask if Mandy came to church, too? Wanted to make a point to see her if she did."

"I'm afraid not," Daniel said. "but I'm not giving up on her coming back yet."

The preacher made a low *hmm* sound then seemed to decide that he had more to say. "Daniel, I know you came back here for Kaden, because you want to be a part of his raising and all, but I've got to tell you, Mary and I have been praying for Mandy nonstop since the funerals."

"I've been praying for her, too," Daniel said.

"The girl had already been struggling with her faith. I remember her senior year of high school she didn't handle it very well when her grandmother passed just three months after her grandfather. Kind of felt like she might have blamed God then, with that being pretty much all the family she had besides her sister.

She'd still come around every now and then to visit the church, but we were losing her. Then when Mia and Jacob died in that wreck, she left the church—and I'm afraid God—completely."

Daniel's mind shot back to that night seven years ago when she'd shown up at his house the week after he had graduated from college. She'd been a senior then, due to graduate from Claremont High just three weeks later. She'd told him that she would be done with school soon, that she was older now and knew exactly what she wanted—to leave the horrible town of Claremont and to live the life she'd dreamed of…with Daniel. Mandy knew he was leaving soon for Malawi, and she wanted to go, too. "I want to see the world, get far, far away from here. Marry me, Daniel, and take me with you."

And Daniel still heard his response. "Mandy, you don't know what you want. You're seventeen years old, and you may not have even met the guy out there made just for you. One day you'll find him and you'll have a real marriage, built on love. Listen, Mandy, marriage isn't something you do just because you want to run away." Then he'd turned and walked away.

Now, as he listened to Brother Henry, he realized that he hadn't been around that year to see how much she'd lost and how terribly she must have been hurting when she came to him that night as her last resort for starting over. Mia and Jacob were already married, and she'd lost her grandparents. Mandy probably felt as if she was all alone, and she'd turned to Daniel…just to be pushed away.

And this past year, her life had been upended again, when she lost more than a sister. She'd lost her only link to family on the day Mia died. The only one but Kaden, that is. No wonder she was so terrified of losing him. Kaden truly was all she had.…

Daniel was jolted back to the present by the sound of Brother Henry's voice. "But, anyway, Mary and I were discussing it last night before our evening prayers, and when we prayed for Mandy, we changed our prayer a bit."

"How's that?" Daniel asked curiously.

"Well, I'll tell you. We've been praying that she'd come back to God, find the faith that she lost, but now we're also praying that she'll find her faith with you." He leaned forward and his voice intensified. "Daniel, I know you came back here primarily for Kaden, but let me tell you, I think God brought you back here not only for Kaden, but also for the kids at this church and for Mandy Carter. I firmly believe you may be the one to save that sweet girl, and I'm praying to God to help you."

Daniel blinked, then swallowed. "I'm praying the same thing."

Chapter Seven

"Wow, that was awesome!" Kaden said, sitting in his booster seat in the back of Daniel's truck. "Did you see the real fish in my room?"

"I did," Daniel said, happy that Kaden had enjoyed church so much.

"It was a visiting fish."

"A visiting fish?"

"Yeah, cause it was day five. Turn on the light, and I'll show you."

Daniel waited until he got to an upcoming red light, then flipped on the interior light in the truck and turned around. "Okay, show me."

Kaden held up his paper, which displayed a big number five, the top of the number filled with a blue sky and birds, and the bottom filled with water and fish. "Day five, day five, God made birds and fish alive," Kaden sang, grinning. "So since it was day five, Ms. Adams brought a fish to visit class." He shrugged. "I guess she didn't have a bird."

Daniel laughed. "Probably not." He turned off the light, waited for the traffic signal to turn green then started up again, while Kaden continued talking about class.

"They've already done the first four days, but I got to be there for day five. And I can go back for six and seven, right?"

"Definitely," Daniel promised.

"Cool, except she said that day six and day seven are on the same night, since seven is a west one."

"A west one?"

"Yeah, I don't know what it means, either, but that was what Ms. Adams said. That day seven was a day of west and so we'll talk about it the same night as day six."

Daniel had to bite his lip to keep from laughing. Then he said, "I think she probably said day of rest, because God rested on day seven."

"Oh, yeah, okay."

"Kaden, do you have a book about creation, you know, a book that tells you about what God made on each of the days?"

"Nope, I don't think I have that one yet."

Funny, out of all of the books he'd put in Kaden's new room today, he didn't remember seeing one on the creation. "I'll get you one tomorrow. I'm pretty sure I have one in my church office. In fact, since you'll be going with me to the church tomorrow, I'll find it and you can look at it while we're there."

"Okay. What else am I gonna do there?"

Daniel had been wondering that very thing. Could he entertain a four-year-old all day at the church building while also getting his work done? He wasn't all that certain he could, but he was going to give it his best shot. "I found some games and puzzles there in one of the classrooms. You can play with those. And there's a television in the office next to mine that you can watch. Lots of movies, too."

"Will we get to have some fun, too, you know, do cool stuff?"

"Yeah, we will," Daniel promised, then wondered what was considered cool that they could do at the church building. He'd figure something out.

"Aunt Mandy lets me cook with her and we build stuff and catch stuff."

Cooking wasn't Daniel's strong suit, but the

building and catching he could handle. "What do you build?"

"Like my wilderness lodge, Lego forts, stuff like that. Sand castles when we're at the beach. And sometimes when it's laundry day, we make a fort with the sheets before we wash them. She lets me help her wash the sheets, too." He paused. "Well, I pour the gooey green stuff on top."

Daniel smiled, realizing that Mandy had found a way to work a four-year-old into her routine. "What about when she takes her pictures? What do you do then?" he asked, wanting to know how Mandy juggled her job and Kaden.

"That's when I'm a big helper. I hold stuff or sometimes I make faces to get the babies to smile. Other times I just kind of play wherever Aunt Mandy goes, but she says that's being a helper, too, cause she needs to concentrate."

Yep, Mandy had definitely perfected the mother role with Kaden. He really did blend into her world. Daniel now quietly prayed that Kaden could blend into his world, as well. It didn't take long to find out that would take a bit of effort and forward thinking on Daniel's part. In fact, it happened within an hour, when Daniel began readying Kaden for bed.

"Brushed your teeth?" Daniel asked as Kaden ran into the bedroom and jumped on the bed. Daniel had done his best to "little boy" the room before Kaden came. He'd bought a comforter covered with an oversize Thomas the Tank Engine & Friends, and had brought a bookshelf from his folks' place that he'd filled with kid books that his mother had kept and stored through the years. It'd been rather exciting to put the books on the shelf and wonder which ones Kaden would select for their nighttime story, since he and Jacob had had these very books when they were Kaden's age.

"Yep, brushed 'em good," Kaden said, opening his mouth for inspection in the same manner as he'd done last night at Mandy's.

"You sure did. So, story time now, right?"

"Story time then prayers," Kaden said, peering around the room as if he was searching for something.

"Here are your books," Daniel said, trying to tamp down on his excitement about the abundance of stories available for Kaden's selection. "Your dad and I read all of these when we were little."

Kaden nodded, but he didn't make a move toward the shelf, and his mouth flattened. "Did you bring my favorite?"

Daniel glanced at the empty suitcase. He'd already unpacked everything, putting Kaden's clothes in the dresser and his toiletries in the bathroom down the hall. Mandy had included some small toys, cars and trucks and Legos, and Kaden's small blue Bible. But no favorite book, and Daniel knew exactly which book Kaden was talking about. "The Moses story?"

Kaden blinked a couple of times and nodded, clearly on the verge of tears. "I read it every night. I *have* to read it every night," he said. "It's my favorite."

Daniel knew that. He just hadn't realized that the particular book was such a critical part of the nighttime ritual. He'd been rather proud of himself for thinking of the bookshelf, but he should have realized that the quantity of books didn't matter. It was the quality of that one story that touched Kaden's heart and finished his day perfectly.

And Daniel didn't have it.

He looked at the clock. *9:05 p.m.* Mandy lived twenty minutes away, and Kaden had already had his bath and was ready for bed.

He really didn't think he should load him up in the truck to go trekking after that book. But then he noticed a fat teardrop land on Thomas the Tank Engine and saw Kaden's quivering lower lip.

"Hang on, slugger. It'll be okay. Let me go call Aunt Mandy."

Kaden nodded, trying to be big in spite of the tears that made him look even younger than four.

Daniel hugged him, kissed the top of his head. "No worries, okay? We'll get the book tonight."

"You promise?"

"Definitely." *God, please let Mandy be willing to help me out here.* Daniel gave Kaden a thumbs-up, ruffled his hair and said, "I'll be right back. Just going to call Aunt Mandy."

"Can I talk to her?" Kaden asked with a sniffle. "I miss her."

Daniel's heart tugged in his chest, but he swallowed and nodded. "Sure. I'll go get my phone."

He snagged his cell phone from the hall table and dialed Mandy. She answered on the second ring.

"Daniel? Everything okay with Kaden?" The worry in her voice was undeniable.

"Yeah, everything's okay, for the most part," he said. "Church went great, and he enjoyed his class."

"Then, what's up?"

"We forgot his favorite book."

"Oh, dear, I can't believe I forgot to pack it. I'm so sorry. Is he going to be okay without it tonight?"

Daniel peeked into the room, where Kaden had flipped over on his side facing the wall, but he didn't have to see Kaden's face to know from his shivering back that he was still crying. "I'm thinking that's a no."

Kaden rolled over, his water-filled eyes wide. "Is that Aunt Mandy?"

"Yep, it is. You wanna talk to her?"

Kaden nodded, lip quivering.

"He wants to talk to you," Daniel said to Mandy.

"Okay, and don't worry. I'm already heading out the door."

"Thanks," Daniel said, truly grateful for her willingness to help him out. "I'd come get it, but…"

"Oh, no, don't do that. He's ready for bed, I'm sure."

"Yeah, he is. Thanks, Mandy." He moved toward the bed. "Here you go," he said, handing the phone to Kaden.

Kaden sniffed. "Aunt Mandy?… Hey, yeah, I forgot it, too." Another sniff, and a swipe of his hand beneath his nose. "Yes, ma'am. I will…. Okay…. Love you, too." He handed the phone back to Daniel. "She's gonna bring it," he said, and thankfully, a slight grin found its way into his waterlogged face.

"That's great," Daniel said. Then he put the phone to his ear to see if she was still on the line, but the line was dead. And Daniel had no doubt that she was probably already in the car.

Twenty minutes later, Daniel heard her car in the driveway. He'd been sitting beside Kaden on the bed, rubbing his back and trying his best to comfort him while they waited on the essential book. "That'll be Aunt Mandy. I'm going to let her in, okay?"

"Okay." Kaden shimmied up in the covers, his eyes heavy but his determination to read the book before sleeping stronger than his need to rest.

Daniel made his way to the front door, opened it and saw Mandy with the book in hand hurrying toward the house. She wore pink-and-red-plaid pajamas with a grey fleece jacket thrown over the top, one feather-trimmed turquoise houseshoe and a red flip-flop. Definitely not the fashion-forward Mandy that he'd always known. Plus, her hair stuck up in the back like she'd been sitting against the headboard. And black smears marred the area beneath each eye.

"Don't say a word," she warned. "I was in a hurry."

"You look adorable," he said.

She'd been stomping up the steps to his front porch, but she paused, tilted her head and studied him. "You mean that."

It wasn't a question, so Daniel didn't answer. Her desire to get here, to help Kaden and consequently help Daniel made her more attractive than if she was decked out in the prettiest outfit in Claremont. And he did mean it, but he hadn't meant to blurt it out. Typically he held his attraction to Mandy Carter in check; he always had, even back when they were teens. But this time, her love for Kaden and her desire to get here threw Daniel off his guard, and the words in his heart sprang free. He cleared his throat and wondered how to get past this awkward moment, but Kaden's yell from his room captured their attention.

"Aunt Mandy? Is that you? Did you bring it?"

Mandy smiled, finished her journey up the stairs and then moved past Daniel. "Yes, honey, I got it!" she answered back. She maneuvered through the living room and down the short hallway to Kaden's room as though she knew exactly where she was going. And then Daniel realized that he'd never even told her where his new home was located. But he'd ask her about that later. Right now, there was nothing more important than getting Kaden his favorite book.

Mandy entered the bedroom and moved to Kaden's outstretched arms. He hugged her tightly. "I missed you, Aunt Mandy."

"Oh, I missed you, too," she said, kissing the top of his head and then holding out the book. She inhaled and grinned. "Smells like you bathed and washed your hair, too."

"I did, and I remembered under my arms and behind my knees."

"Good job."

"And Uncle Daniel helped me rinse my hair, and we didn't get one bit of soap in my eyes."

"That's great," she said, kissing him again. "And here it is, your favorite. I'm sorry I forgot to pack it."

He beamed, no apologies necessary. "Thanks!" Then he looked at Daniel, and all traces of tears disappeared. "Hey, Uncle Daniel, now we can all read it together, right?"

Daniel was grateful to be included in the sentimental moment. "Yes, we sure can."

Daniel pulled up a chair; Mandy and Kaden climbed under the covers.

"I'm a mess, huh?" Mandy whispered.

"Not at all," Daniel said. "And I appreciate you hurrying over. We really needed this book."

"Yep, we really did," Kaden agreed. "So, I'll do the first two pages, right?"

"Right," Mandy said, beaming. Have mercy, she had an incredible smile. She glanced up, caught Daniel staring, but he didn't look away. He couldn't if he wanted to. She looked perfect, snuggled against Kaden in her pj's. Her eyes widened a little, and she mouthed, "What?"

"Adorable," he mouthed back and was rewarded with a slight tinge of pink on her cheeks. Then she jerked her attention to the book in Kaden's hand as though afraid to look at Daniel a second longer. Daniel grinned and also turned his attention to the story.

Kaden opened the book to the first page and repeated in the same manner as last night, "Moses needed someone special to take care of him, because his mommy couldn't. She wanted to find the perfect person to take care of him." He looked up at Mandy joyfully. She returned the tender gesture, and Daniel felt his heart lurch in his chest.

"That's right," Mandy said.

"See, Uncle Daniel, that's his sister, watching to make sure that the princess finds him." Kaden again pointed to Miriam, and Daniel nodded.

Kaden turned the page. "The princess took Moses into the castle and was like his mommy for while he grew up, and Moses was happy that the princess was taking care of him." Kaden looked up to Daniel this time. "Right?"

Daniel fought the lump that had formed in his throat, and he bit back the emotion that came with realizing why this story was Kaden's favorite. "Yes, that's right."

"Okay, you can finish now, Aunt Mandy," Kaden said.

And Mandy completed the story, while Daniel looked at the little boy he loved…and at the princess beside him in the bed.

When she finished the story, Kaden shimmied down farther into the covers. "Time for prayers," he said. "You first, Uncle Daniel."

Daniel cleared his throat, bowed his head. "Dear God, thank You so much for Kaden and for the role that You are allowing me to have in his life. Thank You for letting us enjoy church together tonight, and thank You, God, for allowing Mandy to bring us the book he loves and for letting her stay to tuck Kaden in." He paused, swallowed, and added, "And thank You, God, for opening my eyes tonight. In Jesus's name, amen."

"Uncle Daniel, is something *wrong* with your eyes?"

Daniel chuckled. "No, slugger. They're fine. I just thanked God for helping me understand things better. That's what I meant."

"Oh, okay," Kaden said, but his confused look said he still didn't get Daniel's statement. In any case, he turned his attention from Daniel to Mandy. "Aunt Mandy, your turn now."

Her brows shot up, mouth tensed. "Kaden, I think I just want to listen to you say your prayers tonight."

Kaden frowned. "Don't you want to talk to God, too? Uncle Daniel does. Don't you want to?"

"No honey, not tonight."

Clearly disappointed, Kaden sighed loudly. "Okay, then I guess it's my turn." Bowing his head, he started, "Now I lay me down to sleep. I pray the Lord my soul to keep. If I should die before I wake, I pray the Lord my soul to take. God, bless Aunt Mandy and Uncle Daniel. And thank You for letting me go to church. And thank You for letting Aunt Mandy bring me my favorite book." Kaden's mouth quirked to the side, his eyes still pinched shut. "And God, please specially bless Aunt Mandy so she'll want to talk to You again. In Jesus's name, amen."

Mandy turned toward the wall and attempted to casually dab at her cheeks, so Daniel diverted Kaden's attention. "That was a great prayer, slugger."

"Yours was good, too," Kaden said, then turned to Mandy. "Love you, Aunt Mandy."

She gave him a watery smile. "Love you, too, sweetie."

"You okay?" he asked.

"Mmm-hmm," she said, forcing her smile to stay in place, but Daniel could tell it was an effort.

"Are you gonna stay at Uncle Daniel's, too?"

She cleared her throat and seemed to gain her composure. "No, I need to drive back home, but you'll have a good time staying at Uncle Daniel's house and going to the church with him tomorrow when he works."

"I know. He told me so," Kaden said, while Mandy climbed out of the covers and slid her feet into her odd shoes.

She laughed, kissed the top of his head. "Night, Kaden."

"Hey, don't forget to fluff my pillow," he said, and she proceeded to pound the living daylights out of the pillow, and then proclaimed it ready for a good night's sleep, while Kaden giggled.

"Sweet dreams, Kaden," she said.

"Night, Aunt Mandy."

Then Daniel also kissed him good-night, flipped the switch on the Thomas the Tank Engine & Friends night-light he'd purchased with the bedding and then turned off the overhead light before following Mandy to the front of the house.

"You want a cup of coffee or something before you leave?" he asked. He really didn't want her to go, and he didn't want to analyze why not. "I've got decaf."

"I can actually drink the real stuff right up until I go to bed and still sleep like a log," she said, "but I don't want any." Her cheeks still held a hint of pink from his earlier comment, and she wouldn't look at Daniel, probably because she was embarrassed by his uncharacteristic statement.

"Okay." He rubbed his hand over his worn Bible, perched on the table near the door. He attempted to shift the subject back to something more comfortable for Mandy. "I hope you know how much I appreciate you coming over and bringing that book. He really needed it."

She turned those dark eyes his way again. "I should have packed it to start with," she said, pushing a wayward lock of hair behind her ear and consequently making Daniel wonder just how soft her hair would feel against his palm.

"Mandy, I think I know why he loves that story so much."

"Why?" she asked, and the inquiry in her tone told Daniel that she really hadn't figured it out.

"Because *you* are his princess. You're the one that has taken care of him when his mommy couldn't, like Pharaoh's daughter did for Moses." He smiled. "I always said you were a princess. Turns out Kaden sees you that way, too."

She took a hand to her mouth as she thought about what he'd said. "Do you think that's okay? That he sees me that way?"

Daniel nodded. "Yeah, I do. I think it's great, because he knows that Moses was taken care of and loved, and he knows that he'll be taken care of and loved, too."

"Does it bother you?" she asked, tilting her head and raising her brows. "That he sees me that way?"

"No, not at all. I'm glad that he knows how much you love him."

"But you want to take him away from me," she said. "Or take custody away from me, at least." The pink in her cheeks had disappeared, the magic of the earlier moment erased.

"I never want to take him away from you," Daniel clarified. "And I only want custody because I believe that's what's best for him. If you do stay in Claremont, then nothing will change. You can still see him any time you want." He hated that everything had turned all cut-and-dried again. He preferred it when they were simply two people working together to make Kaden happy, because it was in those rare instances when she let her guard down and let him glimpse the real Mandy.

"It isn't the same, Daniel."

Unfortunately, he believed he knew Mandy Carter a little better than she even knew herself. "I know it isn't, but I'm honestly only trying to give you what you want, a chance to help me raise Kaden but also to leave if your desire to see the world gets too tempting."

"I'm not like I was back then. I don't think I have to run away to be happy." She huffed out a breath. "And the truth is, I didn't run away then."

"Mandy, it's late, and we really don't need to talk about this now. I'm still getting my feet wet in the whole task of raising Kaden." He scrubbed a weary hand across his jaw.

"If you need me to come back over tonight, just call. I'll come right away."

"I know you will," he said, "but we should be okay now. I really appreciate you coming, though. It meant a lot to Kaden, and it meant a lot to me."

She glanced around, took in the framed Bible scripture on the walls, the photos of kids from the church from the past and present. "This house is still the same way I remember," she whispered.

Daniel hadn't realized how she already knew where he lived, but now it all clicked into place. This house had belonged to the church for as long as Daniel could remember and was always used as living quarters for the youth minister. "You used to come here with the youth group, didn't you?"

She nodded. "Not that often, but a few times." She honed in on one of the photos and stepped closer. "There I am."

Daniel looked at the picture, which showcased about thirty high school kids piled up in the back of Carl Cutter's hay truck. Smiles adorned all faces, including the one on the prettiest girl, perched in the middle of a bevy of friends and laughing. "You had pigtails," Daniel said, eyeing the long, shiny brown swirls topped in red bows.

"My grandmother said that the proper attire for a hayride was overalls, pigtails and red bows." Her hand moved slowly above her heart as she spoke. "She said it made her happy to see me so happy that night. That was the fall of my senior year. Mia had already married Jacob, and it was just me, my grandmother and my grandfather living at the photography studio then." She inhaled deeply, eased it out. "My grandfather died two months later, and then my grandmother three months after him. Both were gone before I even graduated."

"Mandy, I'm sorry I hurt you back then. I didn't realize what all you had gone through when you came to me for help that night."

"You mean when I came to you and proposed," she said, shaking her head. "I'm sure you thought I was crazy."

"No, I just thought you wanted to leave town, but I didn't really think about why you wanted to leave so badly."

"It's okay. I wasn't thinking clearly, and everything worked out. If I'd have left then, I wouldn't have been here to spend a few more years with Mia before she died. And I'd never have forgiven myself for that."

Her features softened, and Daniel wanted to hold her and tell her he was sorry that she'd been so hurt in the past, sorry that she'd lost everyone she cared about most. Most of all he wanted to tell her that he would never hurt her again, no matter what happened with Kaden. But he wasn't sure she'd believe him, and he was fairly certain she didn't want him holding her now. As far as Kaden was concerned, he was now the enemy as long as he wanted custody.

So instead, he simply said, "Mandy, everything will be okay. God has a plan."

"But what if I'm not in it," she whispered.

Daniel stepped toward her, forgetting the boundaries of custodial battles and that they might very well be on opposite sides of a courthouse in the upcoming weeks. "Mandy?"

"Yeah?" She looked up, tears gathering at the ridges but not falling free.

"Let me hold you," he said, edging even closer, close enough to smell that peach scent. "I know this is hard, and as difficult to believe as it may sound, I care about you—and I also care about Kaden."

She didn't step into his embrace, but she didn't move away when he eased her into his arms and held her close.

"He needs me, Daniel," she said softly, her voice muffled against his chest.

Daniel was instantly reminded of how

petite she was against his frame, and how extremely feminine. He also realized that in all the years he'd known her, they'd never hugged. Never touched. Now he wondered why. And then he closed his eyes, inhaled her sweet scent and felt the gentle warmth of holding her, protecting her. And suddenly he realized that he didn't want to let go.

Chapter Eight

Daniel didn't really need Mandy along for the trip to the sporting goods store. She'd already said she didn't know anything about the equipment Kaden would need for T-ball, but he thought Kaden would want her to be a part of the trip. But deep down Daniel knew the desire to have her along wasn't entirely about Kaden. Ever since he'd held her in his arms and comforted her last night, he hadn't stopped thinking about how good it'd felt to hold her…and how much he wanted to do that again.

"So was I good today at work?" Kaden asked from his booster seat.

Daniel grinned at him via the rearview mirror. "Yep, you were great." It'd been a lot easier entertaining Kaden at the church than Daniel had anticipated thanks to the fenced-in playground by Daniel's office window and the abundance of space for running throughout the class hallways. Kaden had played all day except for when he'd taken his afternoon nap, which had lasted a whopping three hours. Daniel had actually called Mandy after hour two to ask if that was normal. She'd merely laughed, said Kaden must have been exhausted and then assured Daniel that everything was okay.

Amazing how much he'd enjoyed hearing her laugh and chatting with her about the boy they were raising together. He liked the thought of that, raising Kaden with Mandy, and wouldn't mind it being a permanent arrangement. But he couldn't forget her final words in that email.

It isn't fair, Daniel, that I am stuck here taking on all of the responsibility and you're off on your safaris and whatever else you do. Did you ever think that I might need a little freedom, too? Do you have any idea how hard this is, raising Kaden by myself? Or do you even care? I gave up my dream for Kaden. I love him, but I had a dream, too. I did. I wanted to go everywhere. See everything. And it hurts to know you haven't done a thing to help here and you're still living your dream.

Daniel shook his head to clear the memory. Her words had pierced his heart then. But her statement last night had also struck a chord.

"He needs me, Daniel."

Daniel knew it was true. Kaden did need Mandy. And what's more, Daniel suspected that *he* needed her. too. But could she be happy in Claremont forever, the way she claimed she was now, when on two different occasions she was ready to turn tail and run? And what would it do to Kaden—and Daniel—if she did?

"Hey, this is the way to Aunt Mandy's house," Kaden said, craning his neck to peer down the street ahead. "I thought you said we were going to a store to buy my T-ball stuff."

"We are. You, me and Aunt Mandy are going to buy what you need to play, and then we're all going to the Little League fields to practice." Mandy had been so happy when Daniel had asked her to come along that he'd practically been able to see her smiling through the phone. He'd sure felt it.

"Really? I wonder if Nathan will be there.

I saw him last night at church, but he was in a different class. I'm with the four-year-olds, but he is with the seven-year-olds. And I saw Lainey, too. She's with the two-year-olds. Every class is kind of divided up, so you can't just go with your friends, but that's okay 'cause I still had fun. Hey, I still got my day five paper in the truck. Can I show it to Aunt Mandy when we get there?" Kaden's excited chatter was so fast and intense that he had to suck in a breath at the end.

Daniel laughed. "Sure you can, slugger." He pulled in and parked behind Carter Photography. "I'm sure she'd like to hear about what you learned in class."

Daniel hoped that she liked it enough to want to visit church with them, because he hadn't stopped thinking about Mandy all day, and the fact that she insisted that she was in Claremont to stay. If she was truly here to stay, then they really would be raising Kaden together regardless of who had custody. And if that came to pass, then perhaps Daniel could finally explore his true feelings for Mandy. The only big problem he could foresee with that was her refusal to let God back into her life. Because any relationship that involved Daniel Brantley would unquestionably have God at the center.

Kaden reached over and unbuckled the seatbelt, then crawled out of his booster seat and jumped out of the truck. "Hey, can I go see Aunt Mandy now?"

"Yeah, I'm right behind you."

He heard the door open, and Kaden naturally left it open so that Daniel heard him telling Mandy all about his class as Daniel climbed the back steps. The excitement in his voice warmed Daniel's heart. Stepping inside, Daniel followed the scent of fresh-baked cookies to the kitchen. There he found Mandy sitting at the table already marveling over Kaden's take-home paper. The image of the two of them together was mesmerizing. Mandy, genuinely admiring his artwork, and Kaden, beaming with unabashed pride at her exclamations.

"Kaden, this is beautiful," she said. "Look at how good you are coloring now!"

"The fish were kind of tough, because I wanted the fish to be yellow and orange, and all of the water was blue, and I didn't want blue on the fish. But I messed up on that yellow one, so he's got kind of a green tail."

"You know why?" she asked.

Kaden shook his head.

"Because yellow and blue make green. Tell you what, we'll do a little experiment with colors after you come back home," she said, then amended, "after you come back here."

"Cool!"

Mandy and Kaden continued chatting about colors and fish and birds, then she looked up again at Daniel, still waiting in the doorway. He wasn't sure for what, maybe an invitation to join them? Because he kind of felt like a third wheel. Her eyes warmed toward him, and then she smiled. "There are three plates and three glasses of milk on the table," she said.

Daniel had been so absorbed with watching the two of them that he hadn't thought to count plates. He returned her smile. "It's a good thing, because if you were going to make me smell those cookies and then go without having any, I'd have been one disappointed man."

Kaden laughed, reached for a cookie and dipped it in his milk. "Aunt Mandy wouldn't do that."

"I thought y'all might like a snack after your long workday and before we go shopping," she said.

"We sure do," Kaden said, taking a bite of his cookie. "Uncle Daniel worked at his desk all day, except for when he came out and raced me down the slide. And I played hard all day, except for when I napped."

"I heard you took a good nap," Mandy said, her eyes laughing at Daniel as she spoke.

"Hey, I wasn't sure how long those things were supposed to last," Daniel said, reaching for a cookie.

She tossed the remainder of her cookie in her mouth, licked her fingers and grinned. "It was sweet."

"Thanks." Daniel's eyes found hers and stayed there. She was pretty last night in pajamas, messy hair and mismatched shoes. She was pretty when she was annoyed at him, like when she ran out of gas. And she was pretty now, sitting at the kitchen table and poking fun at him while she ate cookies.

"What?" she asked, catching him staring *again*.

And Daniel could only think of a single word, so he said it. "Adorable."

"Oh, you got the little chocolate chips I like, and they're still gooey in the milk," Kaden said, interrupting the charge of energy overpowering the room.

Daniel wondered if she felt it, too, that powerful pull that made everything around them blur and brought her into perfect focus.

Mandy blushed and then quickly looked away from Daniel to focus on their nephew. "Just the way you like them."

"Watch this, Uncle Daniel," Kaden said, and dipped the cookie in the milk, held it there, then pulled it out and took another bite. Then he pointed to Mandy's face, squished as though she'd bitten a persimmon.

Kaden's laughter rolled out. "She thinks it's gross when I dip it."

"Kaden, I've told you I don't like that word. It doesn't sound nice," Mandy said.

"Right," Kaden said, dipping his cookie again. "Yucky. She thinks it's yucky." He grinned and Daniel laughed when he noticed the chocolate on his front tooth made him look almost toothless.

Mandy noticed, too, and laughed, as well.

"What?" Kaden asked. "Chocolate again?" He smiled big, and chocolate sure enough covered the majority of the top teeth.

"Yes," Mandy said, giggling. "Please take a drink of milk."

Kaden lifted his glass, which now looked

more like chocolate milk than the original white. "I don't think I want to drink it now."

Daniel moved to the sink. "Well, let me get you some water to drink, then." He looked to Mandy. "Where are the glasses?"

"Cabinet to your right," she said, taking a napkin and wiping even more chocolate off Kaden's chin, while Kaden continued to giggle.

Daniel found the glasses, filled one with water and took it to his messy nephew.

After Kaden drank the water and got the chocolate off his teeth, he asked, "Do you dip yours in milk, Uncle Daniel?"

Daniel already had a cookie in hand and dunked it in his own glass of ice cold milk. "Of course."

Kaden smiled and watched Daniel take a bite. "Daddy did, too."

Daniel nodded. "I know. That was our favorite thing to do growing up."

"But Mommy did that," Kaden said, "made that face." He pointed to Mandy, who had that same disgusted look toward Daniel now.

"I'm sorry, I can't help it." She tousled Kaden's hair. "But at least I still make you cookies, even though I know you're going to be gross."

Kaden's mouth fell open and he pointed to her again.

"I meant yucky," Mandy said. "I definitely should have said yucky."

Kaden giggled and reached for another cookie.

Daniel ate cookies, chatted about day five and listened to Kaden describe how he didn't ever want to get out at T-ball, and all the while he kept thinking one thing.

This was very nice.

Chapter Nine

Mandy was so glad Daniel had invited her to go shopping with them today. He could have cut her out of Kaden's life for the next few days, but he hadn't, and for that she was especially grateful. She glanced at the handsome missionary-turned-youth-minister and wondered if he had any idea the effect he had on her and probably on every single woman he encountered. She'd hardly slept a wink last night because she kept hearing a single word from that beautifully masculine baritone. "Adorable." And when he said it again, looking at her as though she was the most beautiful girl on the planet, goose bumps marched predictably down both arms. She ran her palms up and down her arms and hoped that Daniel didn't notice.

Taking her mind from the gorgeous uncle

to the grinning nephew, she attempted to block out whatever was happening between her and Daniel, checked her watch and then tweaked Kaden's cheek. "You know, we had better get over to the sporting goods store. Mr. Bowers closes at five o'clock so we only have a half hour."

"Is that enough time to get all of the stuff I need?" Kaden frantically slid off his chair.

"Sure it is. I know exactly what we'll get," Daniel answered, but he seemed to be looking more at Mandy than Kaden.

Mandy looked away and darted toward her keys, dangling from a hook near the door. "Okay, we should get going, then," she said and hoped her voice sounded somewhat normal instead of excited and anxious and everything else that she was feeling right now toward Daniel.

The three of them went through the gallery, and Mandy flipped the sign on the front door and then locked up so they could walk to the sporting goods shop on the other side of the square. They said hello to folks they met on the sidewalk as they made their way there and stopped for a moment while Kaden laughed at the geese around the three-tiered fountain centering the square.

Mandy had spent every day of her entire life on this square, but there was something different about experiencing it with Kaden and Daniel. This was the first time since her grandparents had passed that she felt like she was part of a complete family. The way people smiled at them, as though they were this young couple with a delightful little boy. Naturally everyone in town knew that Kaden was Jacob and Mia's child. More than likely everyone also knew that she and Daniel were now working together to raise their child. But still, it did feel fairly amazing, the three of them together in the square.

Mandy pictured the First Fridays at the square, when the shops had open houses for the art walk, and the street performers were tucked into every corner. The next First Friday, instead of being confined to her store to give tours and show her work, she'd undoubtedly have Kaden and Daniel there, too. Or maybe by then she'd have hired some help, perhaps Nadia Berry, and Nadia could stay at the store while she and Daniel took Kaden to the kid booths. Her growing excitement about all the possibilities had her feeling almost giddy.

"What's that look about?" Daniel asked, giving her an inquisitive stare.

"I guess I'm just happy," she said and then smiled wider when she realized that was the honest to goodness truth. And at that very moment, Daniel's words from last night echoed in her thoughts.

"Mandy, everything will be okay. God has a plan."

What if He did have a plan? One that involved her and Daniel raising Kaden together? But did she even believe in that anymore? That God would watch out for her and might even help her find happiness? He certainly hadn't done anything about that last year.

Mandy felt the urge to pray, something she hadn't felt in a very long time. Just to ask God to really be there and help her find happiness again. But as she tried to determine how to word her request, she realized that she simply couldn't do it. She couldn't pray, because God had let her down, and she still didn't trust Him to help.

"I'm happy, too!" Kaden exclaimed. "'Cause I'm gonna play T-ball and not get out!"

Mandy was glad for Kaden's interruption in her thoughts, because she smiled and tucked her problems with God away for the time being. Today was about having a good time with Daniel and Kaden, and that's what she was going to do.

"So Mr. Bowers carries baseball stuff at that store, too?" she asked, peering through the shop's windows.

Daniel opened the door for Kaden and shot her a bemused glance. "Baseball is a sport, you know, and there isn't much James Bowers doesn't carry when it comes to sports."

"No, it isn't that I don't think baseball is a sport. I guess I always figured a sporting goods store meant hunting and fishing type of things. You know, outdoor sports."

"Here's a news flash, too, then," Daniel said teasingly. "Baseball is played outdoors."

Kaden laughed loudly, and Mandy shot Daniel her best you-think-you're-funny-don't-you? glare.

Daniel gave her a halfhearted shrug. "Sorry, I couldn't resist. Have you seriously never been in this store, when you've lived your whole life on the square?"

"Why would I have needed to come in here? I didn't fish or hunt."

"There's more here than that, and I wouldn't

have picked you for a hunter, for sure, but I can see you fishing."

"Is that so?" she volleyed back.

"I want to fish," Kaden interjected, entering the shop. "Daddy said he'd teach me."

Mandy and Daniel stopped their banter and looked at the little boy between them. Then Daniel squatted down to eye level with his nephew. "Tell you what. We'll figure out what days you practice for T-ball this Saturday at sign-ups, and whatever days you don't do T-ball next week, we'll go out to the fishing hole Mr. Bowers runs, and I'll teach you to fish."

Kaden wrapped both arms around Daniel's neck. "Awesome," he said, and Daniel kissed the side of his head before standing.

"Mandy, why don't you let me teach you, too?"

"To fish?" She had an instant image of her touching a fish, cold wet scales against her palm, and she winced.

His eyes sparkled with a hint of mischief. "Yes."

"Wow, you're gonna fish, too?" Kaden asked, and Mandy realized that if she was going to raise a boy, she really needed to learn to like little boy things.

"Would I have to bait a hook?"

Amazingly, Daniel's grin got broader. "No."

"I don't know…."

"Aw, come on, Aunt Mandy. It'll be fun!" Kaden said, then yelled, "Hey, look at all that baseball stuff!" He ran deeper into the store without waiting for her response.

But Daniel stood stone still waiting for her answer. "You're considering it, aren't you? Come on, Kaden's right—it'd be fun." He looked toward the man behind the counter ringing up a sale. "Mr. Bowers, is your fishing hole open for business?"

"Why, Daniel Brantley, so good to have you back! I was hoping you'd make it into the store soon. Jolaine and I were thrilled to hear you were taking the job at the church," James Bowers said, giving the other customer his change then walking around the counter toward Daniel and Mandy.

"Our grandchildren will be in that youth group of yours in a few years. And sure, the fishing hole is open. Here's a sheet with the hours of operation, but you can come any time you like." He handed Daniel a lime-green flyer from the counter. "If I'm there when you go, I'll show you where the best spots are. If I'm not there, then Jolaine will be running things, and she can give you the lay of the land." He looked to Mandy. "You gonna fish, too?"

"Would I have to touch a fish?" Mandy asked.

"Not if you don't catch any," Daniel said, which made Mr. Bowers smother his laugh. But when Mandy's brows popped up, Daniel added, "No, no you don't have to touch one. Kaden or I will take your fish off the hook."

"Kaden doesn't need to be near hooks," she admonished.

"Are you going to let me teach him boy things or not?"

"Well, now, this sounds like a discussion that I shouldn't be a part of," Mr. Bowers said. "I'll just head over to the baseball equipment and see if the little man needs any advice." He walked toward Kaden, currently working his way through a colorful array of batting helmets.

"*Well?* I'm waiting for an answer...."

"We're here, aren't we?" She waved a hand around the store, which had an abundance of animals hanging on the wall for a massive *ew* factor.

He grinned. "Yes, we are. So after we get his T-ball schedule and I take a look at my work schedule at the church, I'll let you know what days we'll be fishing next week."

"Oh, joy."

"Are you guys coming?" Kaden yelled excitedly. "They got baseballs and bats and hats and everything! Just like the ones the guys use on TV!"

In less than twenty minutes, Daniel had equipped Kaden with a new T-ball bat, a batting helmet, cleats and a box of baseballs. Kaden was so thrilled about the shiny red batting helmet that he wore it out of the store, which garnered quite a few quizzical looks as the trio crossed the square and then headed behind the shops to get to Daniel's truck.

Mandy opened the passenger door and slid the seat up so Kaden could climb inside. The batting helmet conked the side of the truck on his way in. "Kaden, why don't you take that off until we get to the field?" she asked.

"Nah, I'm in now," he said, jumping into his seat. "I'll keep it on."

Mandy peeked in to see that the top of the helmet hit the roof of the truck, so much that Kaden had to slump in the booster seat to fit. "Kaden, are you sure?"

"Yep, definitely." He sounded just like Daniel. *Definitely.* Daniel said that word a lot, and it was always full of optimism and promise. Hopefully Kaden would be that way, excited about life and his future. Mandy glanced at Daniel, buckling up in the driver's seat, and wondered if Kaden would have the same effect on women as his uncle obviously did.

"Hey, you coming with us, or are you going to stand there staring?" Daniel asked wryly.

A delighted shiver worked its way down her spine as he gazed at her with those Caribbean blues. Yep, an undeniable effect on women, particularly on Mandy.

"Yes, I'm coming." She climbed in while Daniel kept grinning, and she hoped he couldn't tell how happy she was to be riding in this truck with him. Back in high school she'd see the Brantley boys in this old truck, and occasionally Mia would be sitting between them all cozied up to Jacob. Mandy had imagined what it'd feel like to sit in this truck next to Daniel. Granted she was on the passenger side now with a person's width between them. But it still felt almost as good as she'd imagined.

"Oh, hey, I almost forgot. I brought you something." Daniel picked up a small bag by the gearshift and handed it to Mandy. "You can put it on when we get to the field."

Mandy peeked inside the bag, saw a baseball jersey and laughed. "Hold on. If you'll wait a second, I'd like to put it on now."

"Okay," Daniel said.

But Kaden whined, "Aw, Aunt Mandy, can you hurry? I'm ready to get there!"

"I will...I promise." She jumped out of the car, opened the back door to the shop and swapped shirts just inside the door. Then she darted back out wearing a Claremont jersey similar to the one Daniel wore. When she opened the door to the truck, a matching baseball cap was perched on her seat.

"Can't have a jersey without a cap," Daniel explained.

She snatched up the cap, put it on her head and pulled her ponytail through the back hole. Then she took a small step back, struck a pose and asked, "What do you think?"

He looked at her, his eyes studying her for a moment. "I think that jersey never looked half that good on me in middle school. I knew the high school jerseys would swallow you whole, but I found that one and thought it'd work." He looked at her again. "And it does work. Very well, I'd say."

She blinked. So many compliments at one time were an overload, and she wasn't quite used to the giddy tingle that accompanied his words. But she sure could get used to it, especially if the compliments came from Daniel. "This was *your* jersey?"

"You didn't notice *Brantley* sewn on the back?"

"I was so excited that I didn't look at the back. It's number seven?" she asked, trying to peek over her shoulder to see the number on the back.

He visibly swallowed, and his eyes took on an intensity that sent another shiver down her spine. "You remembered my number?"

She'd studied that number on his back for years and had actually dreamed of one day being his official girlfriend and wearing this very shirt. Or the high school shirt. Whatever. Anything of Daniel Brantley's would have done the trick. Now she thought she'd probably said too much.

"What's my number gonna be?" Kaden asked, saving her from answering Daniel's question.

Daniel still looked at Mandy, his attention unwavering, so she glanced toward the backseat. "We don't know what your number will be yet," she said. "But we should find out Saturday, I suppose." She waited a second to try to make sure she didn't look too awkward, then she glanced back at Daniel, still looking at her with a slight smile playing with the corners of his mouth.

"What?" she asked.

"Just thinking that you never cease to surprise me, Mandy," he murmured. "And I mean that in a very good way."

She waited to see if he'd say more, but before he could, Kaden asked, "Uncle Daniel, what number do *you* think I'll get?"

Daniel turned from Mandy to Kaden, thank goodness, and she tried to keep breathing normally.

"Well, if we get a say-so, I'm thinking number ten."

Mandy nodded. *Jacob's number.* "That's a great number," she said. "Mia's favorite number," she added at a whisper. Thankfully she didn't add that her favorite number had always been seven. She'd already embarrassed herself enough with her Brantley boys baseball trivia knowledge.

They drove through town toward the Little League fields with Kaden occasionally popping his hand against his helmet and announcing, "That doesn't even hurt!"

By the time they pulled into the ballpark and found a parking spot, Daniel and Mandy were rolling with laughter at all of the head pops occurring in the backseat.

"Are you sure you got the right size helmet?" she asked Daniel after the two of them climbed out and waited for Kaden to maneuver his top-heavy self out of the truck. "It sure looks big."

"That's because Brantley boys have big heads," Kaden said. "Didn't you hear Mr. Bowers when he said that in the store?"

Mandy laughed so hard she snorted. "Nope, I missed that."

"Because if you'd have heard it, I'm sure you would have added a comment or two," Daniel said.

"You got that right," Mandy quipped, still trying to control her laughter.

"Hey, look, there's some other kid at that field practicing already," Kaden said, pointing to one of the bigger fields in the distance. "Were we supposed to go to that one?"

"No, this is your field." Daniel pulled an old plastic bucket out of the back of the truck and dropped the new baseballs inside, then wedged the bat in, too.

"You sure?" Kaden asked.

"I played here myself when I was your age, so yes, I'm sure. This is the T-ball field."

"You and my dad played here?" Kaden asked.

Daniel smiled down at him. "We sure did."

He picked up the bucket and started toward the field. "Come on, we're wasting daylight."

"Okay!" Kaden said, running behind him, while Mandy took her time following. She enjoyed seeing Daniel and Kaden together, walking toward the field like a father and son. Daniel really was good with Kaden, and she was glad he'd come home to show Kaden little boy things like T-ball.

"You want me to sit in the dugout while y'all practice?" she asked as she passed through the opening in the chain-link fence to enter the field area.

"Are you kidding?" Daniel asked. "You're part of the team. Come on out here." She liked being a part of this team, so she did as she was told.

It felt strange stepping onto the field. As far as Mandy could remember, she'd never been on an actual baseball field. She'd often sat in the stands and rooted for Claremont High. She and Mia had been avid fans, particularly when it came to cheering for Daniel and Jacob Brantley, but never had she had a reason to step foot on the field. Until now. And she was doing so with Daniel by her side and with Jacob and Mia's beautiful little boy ready to learn how to play like his dad and uncle.

Mandy swallowed, emotions she hadn't anticipated creeping in. Sadness at what her sister and brother-in-law had left behind.

"Look, I'm running fast!" Kaden yelled. And he was, flying from home plate toward third, rounding it wide and then heading to second.

"I'm thinking our first lesson is going to be base running," Daniel mused. "And perhaps the order of occurrence in bases." He looked to Mandy obviously expecting to get a laugh, but that wasn't what he found.

Mandy blinked a few times to try to stop the tears. She sure didn't want Kaden to see her cry. So she turned her head the other direction, shielding her eyes as though she were looking at the older child on the minor league field.

But Daniel had seen her and knew better.

"I miss them, too," he said, his words right beside her ear as he moved closer. "But we can't keep Kaden away from what he wants to do because we're battling memories. Besides, those are good memories. Great memories. Jacob and I had some of our best times as a kid on this very field."

She looked up at him and saw that she wasn't the only one with watery eyes.

"I'll be here for you," he said, his rich baritone warming her like butter in the sun. He tenderly pushed a wayward lock of hair behind her ear and wiped yet another tear away. "Tell me you'll be okay, Mandy, because I really don't like seeing you upset."

She nodded, while Kaden crossed home plate from the wrong direction and began yelling "Home run! Home run!" Then she brushed the dampness from her cheeks and smiled. "I'll be okay."

"That a promise?" he asked gruffly.

"Yes, that's a promise," she said.

"Okay, then, let's make this day a good one for Kaden."

Mandy nodded. "Yes, let's do."

He nodded then turned toward Kaden. "I've got three more things for you in my bucket, hiding at the bottom."

"Surprises?" Kaden asked hopefully.

"Yep." Daniel dropped to one knee beside the old white bucket and started tossing baseballs and dropping them on the ground. The bat followed. And then came some plastic bases.

"Is that the surprises?" Kaden asked.

"No, these are bases to use when you practice somewhere else. We won't need them today, since we're at the real field."

"But, like, if there was a game going here, we'd have to go somewhere else and make our own bases and field, right?" Kaden asked, drinking in every word.

"That's right," Daniel said. "But here are your surprises." He withdrew a small square of royal blue fabric and unfolded it to reveal a boys' baseball jersey with a red Rangers logo on the front. Daniel turned it, and the back made Mandy's throat clench tight. Number ten, and above the number the name *Brantley* so big on the tiny shirt that it started halfway down the left side then curved and ended halfway down the right like a rainbow.

"Is that for me?" Kaden asked.

Daniel nodded. "It took me a little digging around in your Maw-Maw and Paw-Paw's attic to find it, but yes, it's for you. This was the one your daddy wore when he was your age. We were on the Rangers for T-ball."

"Wow!" Kaden exclaimed. "Can I put it on now?"

Daniel blinked hard, and Mandy was afraid emotion was getting the best of him. She moved beside him and knelt down by Kaden.

"Sure you can," she said. "I think it's going to fit perfectly." She helped him change shirts and thought she knew why Daniel wasn't speaking; Kaden was the spitting image of Jacob and Daniel when they were his age. Another Brantley boy ready to take on the world.

"How's that?" Kaden asked Daniel.

He nodded, lower lip rolled in.

"Good?" Kaden questioned.

"Very good," Daniel finally said, his voice raw. "And two more surprises."

"Wow! You've brought a bunch!" Kaden looked awestruck as he moved closer.

Daniel withdrew a hat that matched the jersey, put it on Kaden's head and shifted it back and forth until it sat just right. "You'll get a hat at sign-ups Saturday with your team's logo, but this was the one your dad wore."

"Cool!" he said and jumped into Daniel's arms. "Thanks, Uncle Daniel!"

"You're welcome."

Then Kaden wiggled to peer over Daniel's shoulder and see into the bucket. "You gave me *two* more surprise, but you said *three* more surprises."

"Yes, I did." Daniel placed Kaden back on the ground, then turned and pulled the last item out of the bucket. A worn leather glove.

"Hey, is that one for me? I thought I was going to use that." He pointed to the glove Daniel had been toting.

"That one's mine and big for you, but this one should be just right. Let's try it." Daniel held out the glove and waited for Kaden to slide his hand inside. "That looks good from here. Can you wiggle your fingers and make those fingers move, too?"

Kaden stuck his tongue out the side of his mouth and moved the fingers in the glove. Mandy clapped, thrilled to see him so undeniably happy.

"Good job. How do you like it?" Daniel asked.

"It's awesome!"

"Well, it's already broken in and I know for a fact that many a center field ball was caught with that glove."

Kaden gave him a toothy grin and then

looked at the palm, where a name was scrawled in black marker. "What's that say?"

Daniel smiled. "That says Jacob. Your Daddy wrote his name there because that was his glove."

Another jump into Daniel's arms. "I'm sure I'm gonna catch a bunch, too, just like he did."

"I have no doubt you will, but first let's learn a thing or two about running bases and hitting the ball off the tee. Mandy, you know the route for base running, don't you?"

"Yeah," she said.

"Okay, Kaden, Aunt Mandy is going to show you how to run the bases."

Mandy cocked her head. "*I'm* going to show him?"

"I'm trying to pick something you can do for your part of the teaching," Daniel said with a smirk.

"Oh, that was low. Come on, Kaden, I'll show you." She took Kaden's hand and purposefully led him to home plate. "After you hit the ball, you're going to run as fast as you can to first base." She and Kaden ran toward the first base, and Mandy pointed to the cream-colored base. "This is first, okay?"

"Okay!" Kaden yelled and jumped on the base with both feet.

"You will have a coach standing over here," Mandy explained pointing to her right. Then she yelled back at Daniel. "The coach tells him whether to stay or keep going, right?"

He nodded. "And to think I never thought you were paying attention when you came to all of those games."

"Oh, I was paying attention," she said. Not always to the game itself but definitely to the player that was now coaching her and Kaden. She looked at her nephew. "You listen to what the coach says, and if he says go, you'll run to second base, but if he says stay, then you stop right here until he says to go again. Got it?"

"Got it!" Kaden said, scrunching down in a ready position and leaning toward second. "I'm gonna run fast."

"Okay, so let's pretend he said go. Go!" Mandy took his hand and they ran to second with Kaden jumping again on the base with both feet. "And here you look at another coach, and he'll be standing down that way, past third base, kind of by that dugout there. You see?"

Kaden bobbed his helmet-heavy head.

"And that coach will tell you whether to run or whether to stay," she said.

"Hey, Mandy," Daniel called from behind home plate.

"Yeah?"

"I really just planned on you showing him the order to run around the bases. We can probably wait for his coach to teach him who to look at along the way."

Well, why didn't he say that to start with? She thought she was here to teach, and this happened to be something she'd noticed during all her years in the stands. "He could've told us that, huh?" she mumbled to Kaden, who laughed.

"So are we just running now?" Kaden asked.

"I guess so," Mandy said glumly.

"Cool. I'm gonna beat ya!" he yelled and took off toward third.

"Why you little stinker!" She started after him but didn't run full speed and let him round third and head to home, where Daniel waited with two palms stretched out for Kaden's celebratory high five.

"That's a home run!" Kaden yelled.

"Yep, it certainly is," Daniel said. "Except

when you do it for real, you won't be stopping to talk to Aunt Mandy at every base."

"Very funny," she said, slightly winded.

"You gonna make it, old lady?" Daniel asked.

"Hey, now, watch it," she said.

"You let me win, Aunt Mandy, didn't you?"

"I was running," she protested.

Kaden shook his head. "You weren't running very fast, 'cause I could've gone faster."

"Next time, I'm running fast," she said, pointing a finger at him.

"Good, 'cause I am, too!"

Daniel tapped the top of Kaden's helmet. "Okay, little man, let's take a few tries at hitting the ball off the tee. Mandy, can you grab my glove and field them for us?"

She looked at her jeweled wedge sandals, then at the dirty field. Her feet already looked three shades darker than the rest of her skin, and it'd probably get worse.

"Would you rather show him how to bat and let me field?" Daniel asked.

"No," she said, reaching down and unlacing her sandals, then tossing them toward the dugout. "I don't know a thing about how to bat, but I can chase baseballs. You should have told me to wear different shoes, though."

"You knew we were practicing," Daniel reminded her.

"Didn't know I was going to be the entire outfield," she said, but she couldn't hold back her smile. The grass and dirt felt good against her feet, and she truthfully enjoyed every minute of this time with Kaden and Daniel.

"You're loving it," he mumbled, but Mandy heard, and she didn't disagree.

An hour later, after Kaden had mastered the art of hitting the ball instead of the tee, they decided to call it a day. Since Kaden had gotten in some pretty decent hits, Mandy was exhausted from fielding. Sweat dampened her neck and caused her hair to curl beneath the baseball cap. She could only imagine what her face looked like and knew better than to try to find a mirror. She wiped the back of her hand across her forehead. "I'm beat," she admitted, flopping down on the ground beside Daniel and Kaden.

"You're a good player, Aunt Mandy," Kaden said, and just like that, every hot and sweaty minute was worth it.

"Thanks, sweetie."

"There's a vending area over there near the playground." Daniel pointed toward the brick concessions building that centered the ball fields. "Why don't we go grab some bottles of water?"

"Sounds good to me," Mandy said.

"Can I play on the playground while you drink your water?"

Mandy had brought a big Gatorade for Kaden, so he wasn't nearly as parched as Mandy and Daniel. "Sure," she said with a tired smile.

Daniel and Mandy walked to the vending area and purchased two waters, then took a seat at a nearby park bench while Kaden moved promptly to a big tunnel slide and wasted no time shooting through it headfirst.

"What do you think?" she asked, watching Kaden run from the slide to the merry-go-round. "Is he going to be okay? Am, I doing a good job with him?" She hated that she sounded uncertain, but the truth was that raising a little boy was unchartered waters for Mandy, and though she'd been doing her best for the past nine months, sometimes she still wondered if her best was good enough, if her love alone was good enough. And she wondered if Daniel really thought that he could do a better job.

Daniel eyed his nephew then looked at Mandy. "I don't think anyone could be doing a better job, and that includes yours truly. Kaden still thinks about Mia and Jacob, still loves them and mentions them often, but that's what we want, right?" He sighed deeply. "I mean, if he didn't say anything about them at all, we'd be concerned. I think the way you're handling it—the way we're handling it—is just right. We're letting him adjust to the fact that they're gone, but we're also reminding him that they were special and that they loved him more than anything." He took a sip of water, wiped his mouth with the back of his hand. "Is that what you wanted to know?"

"Yeah." She had something else to ask him, but she couldn't decide whether now was the right time or place.

"Go ahead," he said.

"Go ahead with what?"

"Something's on your mind, Mandy. You might as well tell me."

How did he know her so well? "Okay. I do want to know something, and I want you to give me an honest answer."

"I try to always give honest answers. It helps with my chosen profession," he added with a grin.

"Okay, then this one won't be hard. Tell

me, do you still think I'm going to leave? That I can't be happy and satisfied living in Claremont long-term?"

He gave Kaden a thumbs-up as he spun around on the merry-go-round, then took another long drink of his water, his neck pulsing with each swallow. When he finished, he looked at Kaden thoughtfully then turned to Mandy. "I don't know."

"But—" she started, and he held up a hand.

"Let me explain," he said, and she reluctantly closed her mouth and stopped her argument. "I want to make sure I explain this right," he said. "I see you with Kaden now, and you're doing an amazing job. You're the type of mother figure every boy needs. Perfect, I'd say. Your love for him shows with everything you do, there's no denying that. The way you look at him, the way you care for him. But I can't help but remember that you are the same person who couldn't wait to leave Claremont and see the world."

She released a long frustrated breath but allowed him to continue.

"And let's face it, Mandy, you haven't seen much of the world at all. I'm not certain someone as young as you, someone as beautiful as you, would be able to give up on that dream forever."

Mandy wanted to argue, truly she did. But unfortunately there was one portion of his diatribe that claimed dominion over everything else. Daniel thought she was a perfect mother figure. And even more stirring than that, he thought she was beautiful.

She cleared her throat. "I'm not leaving Claremont, because I'm not leaving Kaden. You might as well believe me, Daniel. I'm here to stay."

He'd been watching Kaden again, but he shifted on the park bench and put every bit of his attention on Mandy. She saw those exquisite blue eyes roam her face and she couldn't be certain, but it seemed he glanced a little longer at her lips.

"Daniel, I mean it," she said, and couldn't control the quiver in her voice. "I'm staying."

This time she was certain his attention was on her lips. And this time he said, "Well, for the record, I think you should know that I'm really hoping you do."

That caught her off guard, bringing up a whole new batch of questions. "And if I stay, then what does that do to you wanting custody? Does it change anything?"

He breathed in, eased it out and seemed to contemplate exactly what he wanted to say.

Mandy waited. And waited. She wasn't known for patience, and now proved no different. "Well? Does it?"

"All I can say for certain is—" He paused for a moment, then finished "—that would totally depend on you."

Chapter Ten

Mandy knew Daniel and Kaden were probably at the Little League field again, but she had too much going on at work Friday afternoon to take off again, even though she was dying to find out what Daniel's odd remark meant yesterday afternoon. If she stayed in Claremont—and Daniel said he hoped she did—then Kaden's custody depended on Mandy.

Right after Daniel's peculiar statement, Kaden had finished playing on the merry-go-round and declared he was starving, and Mandy never got another chance to ask for clarification. But a whisper of hope had kept a smile on her face all day.

Did Kaden's custody depend on Mandy because Daniel was experiencing the same feelings as Mandy when they were together? Was he thinking about a future with her? A future where custody wouldn't matter because they would be together—really together—in every sense of the word? Was he maybe even thinking about spending his life with Mandy?

She closed her eyes and easily pictured her mouth on his, kissing Daniel the way she'd often kissed him in her dreams, with affection and love. And she just as easily pictured that kiss in a church with Mandy in a white gown, Daniel in a black tuxedo and all of Claremont cheering them on as they began a new life together with that one perfect kiss.

"Miss Carter?"

The timid sound of her name caused her eyes to open and the dream to evaporate. She'd called Nadia Berry last night and offered her a job working three hours after school each day at the studio. Today was her first day, which was one reason Mandy couldn't go to the Little League field. She needed to train her new employee. Now that employee stood at the entrance to the studio room where Mandy had been working and looked like she shouldn't have intruded.

"I'm sorry," Nadia said with a soft smile. "I finished sorting the photos in the front and wanted to know what you needed me to do next. I didn't realize you were praying."

"No, I—" Mandy shook her head "—I wasn't praying." What an odd thing for the girl to assume. But Mandy supposed some people prayed throughout the day. Daniel probably did. But at Nadia's confused expression, she added, "I was just…thinking."

"Oh, okay," Nadia said. "Well, I'm sorry to interrupt while you're thinking."

"It's fine. No problem," Mandy said, standing. "I didn't realize how quickly you'd get those photos sorted."

"I divided them up into individual folders on the computer and named them by the person's last name and then the date of the photos."

Mandy's eyes widened. "I've been meaning to do that but haven't had the time." Actually she had the time, if she'd have spent less time with Kaden over the past few months, but organizing the files on her computer hadn't been her priority. Raising Kaden was. "Thanks, Nadia. That's awesome."

"You're welcome," she said shyly. "I spend a lot of time on the computer at home and even help Dad with some of his files and things, organizing them and making spreadsheets, things like that." Her father, Anthony, was a plumber and probably had plenty of customer files to organize. The fact that Nadia was already familiar with such things was a big plus to her abilities assisting Mandy in the afternoons.

"And to think, I thought I was mainly hiring you to answer the phone and tend to customers when I'm gone on photo shoots. Little did I know, you're going to run the place better than I could."

Nadia's smile went full bloom now, and Mandy realized she was even prettier with that big bright smile.

"Thank you, Miss Carter," she said.

"You're welcome. And you can call me Mandy." She was only eight years older than Nadia and wasn't all that comfortable with the formal use of her name.

"Okay, I will," Nadia said. "So what do you want me to do next?"

"If you've got those files separated, you can start emailing the past week's photography customers with links to their photo proofs and with information on how they can place their order on my website. There's a standard email that I use," Mandy said.

Nadia nodded. "I saw it on the desktop. Where do I find the customer emails?"

Mandy told her and then beamed as Nadia

headed back to the front of the gallery to continue working. She couldn't imagine why she hadn't hired an assistant before. Nadia was a fast learner and observant. She would be a huge help to Mandy, enabling her to do more shoots away from the studio. And Mandy could attend more T-ball games with Kaden. She blushed. And with Daniel.

Mandy turned her attention back to the photos she'd added to her portfolio for the Alabama State Photography Contest. Winning the contest would put her in some of the best galleries in the southeast so she wanted to make certain this portfolio shined. The bell on the gallery door sounded, and Mandy left the photos and started toward the front of the store to see if Nadia needed help. She had faith that the teen could answer customer questions, but since this was her first day on the job, Mandy wanted to make sure she was comfortable in that part of her position.

Mandy entered the gallery to find a boy in a maroon-and-gray Claremont High baseball uniform standing across from Nadia at the front desk. From Mandy's vantage he was turned to the side, but she noticed long light brown hair ruffled out from his cap, broad shoulders filled out his uniform and a strong jaw line showcased a ruggedly handsome face. A Cutter for sure.

"I didn't know you were working here," he said to Nadia, who glanced up through long black lashes at the tall teen.

"Today's my first day," she said softly.

"I told my brother I'd come by here today," he said, "make an appointment for senior pictures. So I wanted to come before I have to be at the field."

"I can make an appointment for you," Nadia said shyly. She moved her fingers across the computer keys, and Mandy noticed that her hands were trembling slightly. The boy, undoubtedly Casey Cutter, didn't seem to notice. He seemed too intent on holding his chest out and beaming at Nadia anytime she'd look up.

"Hello," Mandy said, strangely feeling like an eavesdropper in her own gallery. "Can I help you?"

He cleared his throat, tore his attention from Nadia and grinned at Mandy. Deep dimples bracketed both sides of his smile, just like his older brother.

"I'm Casey Cutter. My brother John said he talked to you about maybe coming out to our farm and taking some pictures."

"He did," Mandy said.

"The thing is," Casey said, "I have baseball practice or games every day during the week and most Saturdays. Would there be any way you could come to the farm Sunday afternoon? That's what John wanted me to check on."

Nadia looked up from the computer. "Oh, Sundays aren't on the schedule here." She looked at Mandy. "Do you work on Sundays, between church times?"

Mandy swallowed. The girl assumed Mandy went to church somewhere and that she prayed often. Little did she realize, Mandy had done neither since Mia died. Instead of explaining, she smiled and said, "Yes, Sunday afternoon would be great." She'd let Daniel take Kaden to church Sunday morning the way he wanted, and then Daniel could spend Sunday afternoon with him, too, while she took Casey's photos. She might as well get used to sharing Kaden. "This Sunday okay for you, Casey?"

"Yes, that's fine," he said.

Mandy nodded, looked to Nadia. "Can you add that to the schedule on the computer, and you can add Sunday afternoons from now on, okay?"

"Okay," Nadia said, smiling at Mandy then blushing at Casey. "I'll put you down for Sunday," she said to him, but her eyes had returned to the computer.

"Sounds good," he said, then stood there a moment before clearing his throat and asking, "So, um, how do you get to work here after school? Did you get a car?"

"No, that's what I'm working for. I want to save for a down payment. Dad said if I get the down payment saved, then he'll help me get a nice used car at the end of the summer."

Casey nodded, and Mandy busied herself with the stack of mail, flipping through the bills while he continued to talk to Nadia.

"So someone drops you off here and picks you up?"

"Oh, yes," Nadia said, apparently embarrassed that she didn't answer the question. "My mom or dad brings me and picks me up."

Another nod of his baseball cap, then he said, "Well, you know, I have baseball practice or a game right after school every day, but maybe if you needed a ride home from work I could, like, pick you up and take you home if that would help your folks out and all."

Nadia's dark eyes lifted. "Okay, that'd be nice."

He controlled his smile, but Mandy could

tell he was thrilled. "So I guess I will check with you and see if you need a ride home sometime?"

"Okay," she said, her hands now completely still on the computer keys.

He released more of that dimpled grin, and then glanced at Mandy. "What time would you want to take the photos Sunday?"

"You know, why don't we wait until later in the day, around seven o'clock, so we can take advantage of twilight and sunset?" Mandy asked.

"I'll be ready," he said, then to Nadia, "And I'll check with you next week about taking you home."

"Okay."

Casey Cutter turned and strutted—that was the only way to describe the confident swagger—out of the gallery. And Mandy waited until she saw his pickup drive away before she beamed at Nadia.

"I think you may have an admirer," Mandy said.

Nadia's head shook slightly, but the corners of her mouth curled. "Casey?"

"Yes, Casey."

Still shaking her head, Nadia said, "I don't know. I mean, he talks to me some, and he asked if he can take me home from a ball-game sometime, and now take me home from work, but…"

"But what?"

Nadia put a hand to her mouth to cover her grin, so her words were even softer than normal. "But he's so cute. And popular. All the girls think so."

"Looks to me like he's got his eye on one girl," Mandy said. "I'm just saying…"

Nadia dropped her hand and laughed. "My mother thinks so, too, but I didn't, well, I didn't want to get my hopes up. You see… he didn't used to go to church at all—and it's important to me that whoever I end up dating is a believer. But Casey has started coming back to church and he's started acting, you know, like he's a Christian. I mean, he still tries to act all tough and everything around the guys, but when he's at church or when it's just me, he really seems like he's different."

"Different in a good way, I take it?" Mandy asked, and was suddenly back when she was sixteen and swooning over Daniel Brantley every time he'd come home from college. The feeling wasn't all that different than the way she felt every time she was around him now.

"Yes," Nadia said. "I mean, I always thought

he was the cutest boy at school, but when I figured out, you know, that he's good, too, that his tough-guy thing is kind of an act or whatever, well then that made him even cuter." She sighed. "I tried to explain it to my mom, and she said that she got it, but it sounds weird, huh?"

"No," Mandy said. "I get it, too." Daniel's "good" factor always made him even more appealing in Mandy's eyes, too, even if at times she was a little jealous that he found it so easy to put his faith in God and she simply couldn't.

"I'm sorry," Nadia said with a grin. "I'll get back to work instead of talking." She paused. "You know, if you're taking the pictures later on Sunday, he'll miss the evening church service. You both will."

Mandy nodded, not knowing what to say. Then she cleared her throat and said, "I really think the photos will be better if we take them at twilight."

"Yeah, it's just sad you're both gonna miss church, though. I didn't think of it when he was here, or I'd have asked him if he wanted to wait until another time." She lifted one shoulder in a mini shrug. "I told my mom, too, that I can't think all that well when

Casey is around. I mean to say lots of things, but nothing comes out."

Mandy laughed. "Totally understand. And after he gets his portraits done, chances are he won't be dropping in very often," she said, walking back toward the studio, then she called over her shoulder, "except when he gives you a ride home." She heard Nadia's self-conscious laugh as she continued down the hall and was glad that she'd been able to get out of the church conversation fairly easily. When she reached the studio, her cell phone rang.

"Hello?" Mandy answered.

"Hey, it's us," Kaden said.

She smiled. "Hi, us, what's up?"

He giggled. "Uncle Daniel said you would want me to tell you about how I did with practicing today."

"He's right," Mandy said, again glad that Daniel was including her in his one-on-one time with Kaden. "So how did you do?"

"I got a, wait a minute, hold on. Hey, Uncle Daniel, what's it called again?" Mandy heard Daniel's deep voice answer and then Kaden continued, "A grand slam."

"A grand slam! Wow!"

"Yeah, well, it wasn't like a real one, since

I hit the ball and there wasn't real runners on the bases, but since we were pretending there were runners and since I hit it real hard and ran real fast, I got a home run and when the other guys are on all the bases and you get a home run, it's a grand slam. And that's the best you can do."

"Well, that's awesome!" Mandy said.

"Yep, it is. And Uncle Daniel said he needs to talk to you, too. He's wanting to take you to practice how to—what? Oh, wait, he wants to tell you. Just a minute."

Mandy heard the phone rustling as Kaden apparently handed it over to his uncle. Then Daniel's voice filled the line.

"Hey."

A single syllable, and yet it sent a frisson of anticipation through her senses. "Hey, yourself," she said. "So what are you going to take me to practice?"

"Fishing," he said. "If you're going to get a handle on all of the little boy things, you're going to have to learn how to fish. And I thought I'd teach you tomorrow when Kaden goes over to Chad and Jessica's house to play with Nathan. That way when we all go together, you'll already know the ropes."

"You could just teach me when we take

Kaden," she said, hoping that he'd tell her what she really wanted to hear.

Daniel didn't disappoint.

"Yeah, I could, but the truth is—" he lowered his voice "—that I really want to spend time alone with you."

Her hand moved to her mouth, and she held her smile.

"Mandy, what do you say? Spend the afternoon with me tomorrow?"

She slid her hand away. "Fishing, right?"

"Fishing. And talking. And seeing where things stand."

"With Kaden's custody, you mean?" she asked.

"That, too, but primarily, seeing where things stand with you…and me. I'd like to get to know you better, Mandy."

"I'd like that, too," she finally answered. "I'd like that a lot."

Chapter Eleven

"Looks like I'm the newest Little League coach in town," Daniel said, driving toward James Bowers's fishing hole with Mandy. He waited for her to respond. She'd been very quiet since they'd dropped Kaden off at Chad and Jessica's house, and Daniel now wondered if she'd changed her mind about spending time alone with him and seeing exactly what was going on with their feelings. Then again, maybe he was the only one feeling anything. "Mandy, did you hear what I said?"

"Huh?" She shook her head. "No, I guess I didn't. I'm sorry. I was trying to remember whether I put in another set of shoes for Kaden. I wasn't thinking about him wearing his cleats to sign-ups this morning when I got his things ready for this afternoon. And I meant to put his tennis shoes in his backpack, but I can't remember putting them in."

Daniel glanced at her, her pretty brows puckered as she apparently replayed getting Kaden's things together. She was beautiful. And sweet. And a great mom. He had always been captivated with Mandy's beauty, had actually thought it to be some sort of cruel joke that God would make Daniel so attracted to someone so obviously wrong for him.

But the joke was on him now, wasn't it? Because Daniel didn't want to do anything but be with Mandy now, listen to her thoughts, watch her laugh, make her smile. Today was a chance to get to know each other better, but to do that, he needed her to stop fretting about Kaden's shoes.

"Why don't you call Jessica and ask if the shoes are there? That'd make you feel better, wouldn't it?"

She wasted no time reaching for her purse and pulling out her phone. "Yes, it would. Do you think that'd be okay?"

Bless her heart, trying so hard to do all the right things when it came to Kaden. "I think it'd be fine."

She nodded, quickly dialed the number and began talking to Jessica. From what Daniel could tell on this end of the conversation, yes, Kaden had his shoes and yes, he was having a great time playing in the backyard with Nathan and Lainey. Daniel suspected that was really what Mandy wanted to know, that Kaden was doing fine.

She hung up the phone and looked relieved. "He has his shoes."

"Awesome, so now I guess I'll give my attempt at small talk—and a bit of bragging—another try." He cleared his throat. "So, it looks like I'm the newest Little League coach in town."

Mandy laughed. "And the most modest."

She turned in the seat to look at him while her ponytail whipped behind her in the breeze of the open window. She wore a blue-and-white sleeveless gingham shirt, cuffed denim capris and tennis shoes. He'd been thankful she hadn't chosen any of her fancy sandals, because they wouldn't have stood a chance on the dirt-covered fishing bank. Mr. Bowers had a decent fishing hole, but it could get rather muddy at times sitting on that bank.

"A *bit* of bragging?" she continued.

"Hey, I didn't say I was the best coach. I just said I was the newest."

Her smirk slid into a grin. "I guess you

are, aren't you? Kaden sure was thrilled when Chad and Mitch asked if you wanted to coach a team. And even more when he found out that you were going to be the Rangers. I don't think he stopped smiling after they announced the team's name." She paused, raised a brow. "You didn't have anything to do with getting that particular team, did you? Or with him getting number ten?"

"I'll say this—it didn't hurt that I used to play ball with every member on the Little League board or that they want me to play on the Men's League team."

"Or that you were probably the best player Claremont High ever saw," she added, then clamped her mouth shut as though she'd said too much. And she probably had, because knowing she thought so sent a big surge of male ego soaring, and undoubtedly produced a bigger-than-necessary smile on Daniel's face.

"Hey, don't get all conceited about that," she warned.

"Wouldn't think of it," he said, but still couldn't stop the grin.

"A big head isn't a good quality for a youth minister," she pointed out, nodding as though this was a well-known fact.

"Yeah, but according to Kaden, all of the Brantley boys have big heads." He shrugged. "I can't help it—it's a family trait."

"You're terrible."

"I'm thinking that you may not mean that in a bad way," he said, pulling into the grassy field by Mr. Bowers's fishing hole.

Mandy gazed out toward the oversize pond, bigger than Daniel remembered. Matured willow trees leaned out to create gorgeous shady areas over moss-covered banks. Between the patches of moss, thick lavender ground coverings stretched toward and away from the water. And within all of that, bright red, yellow and pink tulips sprouted in patches that made the scene look like something out of one of Gina Brown's picturesque paintings.

"*This* is the fishing hole?" she asked.

"Trust me, I'm as surprised as you are," Daniel admitted. "It sure wasn't like this when I was in high school."

A man fished with his children on the far side of the lake and a couple of families picnicked on patchwork quilts beneath the willows, which only added to the perfection of the setting.

"Wow," Mandy whispered.

Daniel and Mandy hadn't even gotten out of the truck before the door to Mr. Bowers's cottage office opened and Jolaine Bowers, his sweet-natured wife, stepped out on the porch waving.

"Hello, Daniel," she said. "James told me you were back in town and bringing Mandy to fish today. It's great to have both of you here. He had to run to the square to pick up a few things from the store, but he'll be right back. Y'all can head on out and find you a nice spot to fish." She smiled. "James and I like that shady flat area under the first willow. The ground is soft for me, and there's an old stump beneath the water about midway in the tree's shadow that likes to play house for the crappie, or that's what James thinks."

"Sounds good," Daniel said.

"I've got cold sodas and water in the store here if you need something to drink. And I've also cooked a few things if you haven't eaten and want something for a picnic. That's what most folks do nowadays."

Mrs. Bowers was known for her cooking. Chicken fingers were her specialty. And her desserts were pretty amazing, too, particularly her chocolate pie and her banana pudding, both of which were traditionally piled high with fluffy white meringue. In fact, she was known for pretty much everything she cooked, especially at the church fellowship meals.

"You have chicken fingers in there?" Daniel asked.

"Of course," she said, her dimples popping into place with her smile. "And I just pulled a chocolate pie out of the oven."

"Then I believe you might be able to coax us into an impromptu picnic later—" Daniel looked to Mandy "—if that's okay with you. I'd planned to go somewhere and eat after we finished fishing, but we could picnic here if you like."

Mandy looked at the large cooler labeled Live Bait perched on the side of the building. "Do you have hand sanitizer, too?"

Daniel laughed loudly. "This is going to be fun."

"Yes, dear, I have plenty. And good ol' soap and water, too, if you'd rather."

"Then, yes, I think a picnic will be great."

"And speaking of those fish, I'm going to need to get a bucket of crickets, Mrs. Bowers," Daniel said.

Mandy's hand flew to her throat and her face made the same expression he'd seen when he and Kaden dipped their cookies in milk. "I do *not* want to touch a cricket."

Daniel continued laughing, but Mrs. Bowers said, "Don't blame you a bit. I say if a man wants a woman to go fishing, then he's gotta be willing to handle all the yucky stuff. You're just here for the pretty scenery and the nice breeze off the water…isn't that right?"

"Yes," Mandy said. "That's definitely right. But I have to tell you, if I'd known how gorgeous it was out here I'd have come years ago. Maybe not to fish, but definitely to hang out by the lake and take photos."

"It wasn't like this years ago," Daniel said.

"He's right," Jolaine said, chuckling. "It wasn't much to look at a few years back. But as James started spending more and more time out here at the fishing hole, I decided if I was going to see him during our retirement years, I might as well learn to spend more time here, as well. But an old hole in the ground in the middle of a bunch of dirt wasn't all that appealing, so I put a woman's touch on it, and James actually likes it. Or maybe he likes the fact that his visitors have tripled since I fixed up the place." She winked. "Seems people will come a whole lot more often if they've got something to look at and something to eat when the fish don't bite."

"*Are* the fish biting?" Daniel asked.

"Oh, biting up a storm," she said with a wave of her palm. "It doesn't hurt that James has been stocking the lake for nearly two decades now. Some folks say there are fish in there as big as your leg."

Mandy's hand went to her throat again.

"Oh, don't worry, child. I'm fairly certain that's an exaggeration. Unless they're talking about the catfish. You never can tell about those catfish." She smiled again, pointed to a stack of quilts on a shelf by the door. "Help yourself to a blanket. And you can get a bucket of crickets over there, Daniel. Just pay James when he gets back. He likes to think that he's the money man," she said with a giggle then disappeared inside the shop.

Daniel grabbed a blue-and-cream colored quilt from the stack. "This one looks good, don't you think?"

"Yes, it does."

The door opened and Mrs. Bowers peeked back out. "Mandy?"

"Yes, ma'am?"

"I'll probably go pick up the grandkids when James gets back, so if I don't get to see you again before y'all leave, I wanted to make sure and let you know how much we've missed you at church. You come back any time you like, you hear?"

"Thanks," Mandy said, but made no promises.

The woman's brows knitted slightly, but she gave Mandy a kind smile and said, "Well, we'd sure love to have you back," then she ducked into the shop again.

Daniel and Mandy walked to the edge of the lake and then toward the willow tree, neither of them saying a word about the kind woman's request for Mandy to return to church. Daniel knew that God had put it in Mrs. Bowers' heart to ask, because that was exactly what Daniel had hoped to find out today. He now suspected that Mandy truly wanted to stay in Claremont and raise Kaden, but what he didn't know was whether she planned on allowing God into her life for that endeavor.

Mandy waited while he put the bucket of noisy crickets and the fishing poles on the ground then handed her one side of the quilt. They let it catch the breeze, guided it to the ground and sat on the soft fabric.

"What's on your mind?" He thought he

knew, but he really wanted Mandy to broach the subject.

She rubbed her palms across the floral patches on the quilt and didn't look at Daniel. "I don't want to talk about it now, Daniel. It upsets me when people try to get me back to church, and I know that the missionary in you makes you want to talk about it now that Mrs. Bowers mentioned it. But can we not talk about it today?"

She looked up, dark eyes displaying a plea for him to hold off on the tough questions that he'd been planning to ask. The questions that he had to have answered in order to know whether he could have the future he now believed he wanted with Mandy. He yearned to have a deep, heartfelt discussion about the pain of the past and about how God could help her move beyond that pain, but Mandy didn't want to talk about that today, and Daniel wasn't about to ruin the opportunity to grow closer to her by preaching to her all afternoon.

"Okay, we don't have to talk about it," he agreed.

"Thank you," she said throatily, and he saw that her eyes brimmed with unshed tears.

"Oh, Mandy, come here." He scooted toward her on the blanket, wrapped an arm around her and eased her head against his chest. Then he stroked a hand down her ponytail and enjoyed the silky texture against his palm. She was so sweet, so precious and so afraid to accept God's help, to accept His love.

God, help her learn to let You in, and please Lord, if it be Your will, have her let me in, too. I care for her, God. I'm fairly certain I'm falling in love with Mandy. But I need You there, too. You know that. Be with her now, and let her find a way to mend her heart from the pain of the past. Help her find her way back to You.

Mandy tilted her head, looked up at him and her eyes looked a little clearer. "You said you wanted to get to know me better."

Finally. He could actually feel her relaxing in his arms. "Yep, that's what I said," he said, and smiled. "So let's get started. Mandy Carter, I'm Daniel Brantley. It's nice to meet you."

She pushed away from him and poked his chest. "Very funny. Okay, smart aleck, how do you want to go about getting to know me better?"

"Like this," he said, reaching for a fishing pole.

"Fishing?"

Daniel nodded. "Don't worry. I'm going to bait your hook."

"Oh, I never doubted that."

He laughed. "And each time I catch a fish, you have to tell me something I don't know about you."

Her dark eyes squinted suspiciously. "And each time I catch a fish?"

"I have to tell you something you don't know about me."

"I'm not so sure this is going to be fair." She eyed the water, where they could actually see several big fish swimming within the shadow of the willow tree.

"Why not?"

"Because this is my first time to fish. You've been fishing your whole life, I'm sure."

"You have a point," he said. "So we'll even the odds. For every fish you catch, I tell you something, and for every two fish I catch, you tell me something."

She tilted her head as she considered his offer then nodded. "Deal."

"Now this is good ol' cane pole fishing. You drop your line in the water, watch the bobber and yank the rod up when the float goes under." He grinned. "Pretty, easy, don't you think?"

"As long as you're the one putting on the crickets and taking off the fish, then, yes, piece of cake," she said, sliding off her tennis shoes, then pulling off her socks, as well. Hot pink glitter-embellished polish tipped each of her toes.

"Why are you taking your shoes off?"

"Just seems like if you're going to fish, you should be barefoot. Every picture I've ever seen of kids fishing, they were barefoot, so if I'm going to do it, I'm going to do it right."

"When it comes to the bare feet, you mean, but not when it comes to baiting the hook and taking off the fish."

"My willingness to conform only goes so far," she said, and Daniel laughed. Heaven help him, she was fun.

"All right, well, here's your pole." He handed her the end of the rod. "Hold it right there a minute while I bait the hook."

She looked away. "Tell me when you're done."

He laughed, put a cricket on her hook. "Done."

She glanced back with one eye open and squished her face at the messy cricket. "Ew. Big-time ew."

"You won't see it once you put it in the water," he assured her.

She promptly flung the pole toward the water and nearly let go in the process. Daniel jerked toward her and grabbed it in the nick of time.

"Hang on there, we're cane fishing. Not quite so energetic."

"I thought there was casting involved," she said.

"Casting? What do you know about casting?" he asked, baiting his own hook.

"I used to watch Bill Dance with Granddaddy," she admitted.

"You watched Bill Dance? So you *do* know about fishing," Daniel accused.

"I know about it. Doesn't mean I actually participated. But I do plan to catch a few and learn a few things about my fishing partner," she said and turned her eyes on her bobber. "Come on fishie, fishie, gobble up that cricket."

"A minute ago I thought you felt sorry for the cricket," he said, finishing his hook and plunking it in the water not far from hers.

"Nah, I just didn't want to see it on the hook," she said, as her red-and-white float disappeared beneath the water. "Hey, I got a bite!" She yanked the rod and pulled up a nice-size bream. "Look! Look!" she yelled, dangling the fish right in front of Daniel's face. "I got one!"

He moved his own pole to the ground and pushed it under his leg to hold it in place, then caught the swinging fish. "Yep, you sure did." He took the fish off the hook, tossed it back in the water and said, "For someone who's never fished, it sure didn't take you long to get the hang of it."

"I paid attention when Granddaddy and I watched his fishing shows," she said smugly. "So, a deal's a deal. Tell me something."

"Something," he quipped, reaching for the cricket bucket and getting another one for her hook.

"Very funny. We made a deal, and you have to tell me something I don't know about you."

"Okay," he said, releasing her baited hook. "I thought about playing baseball in college. Or I guess I should say that I turned down the chance to play baseball in college."

She dropped her line in the water, but her eyes never left Daniel. "You mean you got a scholarship to play baseball?"

He nodded and pointed to her bobber, which had gone south…again.

Mandy yanked it out of the water, but she waited too long. The cricket was gone, but there was no sign of a fish.

"You weren't fast enough," Daniel said.

"That's okay," she said, moving the hook toward his face. "You can bait it again. What do you mean you turned down a scholarship. Where to?"

"Alabama."

"No way!"

"Yes," he said, smiling. "Way."

"Why?" she asked, while he stuck another unlucky cricket on her hook.

"Because it wasn't what I thought God wanted me to do. I wanted to go to a Bible college and follow my folks' lead into mission work. They waited until Jacob and I graduated high school, then they left to go and spread God's word in India. After I visited Malawi on that mission trip as a freshman in high school, I knew that's where I belonged." He shrugged. "So I passed up the baseball scholarship."

"Ever regretted it?" she asked.

"Not once," he said, as his bobber headed beneath the water. He pulled it up and smiled at the decent-size crappie on the end of the line. "That's one." He held up a finger.

"Takes two," she said, holding up two.

"But I'm halfway there," he reminded.

She rubbed her nose. "Was that a rain-drop?" Then she glanced toward the water. "Oh, look!"

And while they watched, the water pebbled toward them as a gentle spring rain eased its way across the pond.

"I've never actually *seen* the rain coming before!" she said. "Look at it!"

"I am," he said, "but as nice as it is right now, I have a feeling it's probably going to pick up steam as it gets going." He pointed toward the opposite side of the pond, where the family that had been picnicking now sprinted around the water's edge to get back to their vehicle.

"Oh, wow, it is coming fast, isn't it?" she said, and pulled her line out of the water... with a fish on the end. "Look!"

He laughed. "I see. Give it here and I'll set him free."

The rain did get harder, so he wasted no time getting the fish off the line and tossing it back into the water.

"Tell me something else," she said, not

making an effort to even put her shoes on until he gave her what she was due.

Daniel pushed damp hair from his forehead. "Something you don't know about me?"

Water streamed down her face, and she wiped it aside and nodded. "That was the deal."

"Okay, then. I've always thought you were the most beautiful girl I've ever seen."

Her mouth fell open, and Daniel's bobber disappeared again. He reached down, pulled up yet another fish, freed it and tossed it in the water.

"Your turn, Mandy," he said, raising his voice a little to be heard above the rain steadily pounding the water and the crickets chirping wildly in the bucket. "Tell *me* something I don't know about you."

She blinked several times, raindrops getting even harder now, and still made no effort to move.

Daniel placed the poles on the ground and stepped toward her. "I'm waiting, Mandy."

"That night," she said, her words also muffled by the rain beating all around them, "when I came and found you, and I asked you to marry me and take me away..."

Daniel's heart thundered in his chest. "Yes?"

"I knew you didn't love me." She bit her lower lip, looked into his eyes and visibly swallowed. Then she added, "But I prayed that you'd learn to."

"Oh, Mandy," he said, and in spite of the fact that they were drenched completely and the rain was coming down harder, Daniel pulled her close, tilted her face to his and said, "I shouldn't have turned away from you then."

"You didn't love me."

"I didn't think you knew what you wanted," he said hoarsely.

She wiped wet bangs from her eyes. "You were probably right. I didn't know what I wanted. I thought I did, but mainly I wanted you to be there for me, to help me through the hardest time in my life and maybe to eventually love me."

He left the fishing rods on the ground, took her hand and moved beneath the willow to shield them from the now-pouring rain. "What about now, Mandy?" he asked. "Do you know what you want now? Because I know what I want."

"What do you want, Daniel?"

"I want you to give me another chance." He tenderly slid a finger beneath her chin, moved his face to hers and brushed his mouth across hers in a sweet, tender kiss. Her lips were soft, warm and perfect. Daniel lost himself in the joy of kissing Mandy.

He wanted to hold her here forever, to protect her from any pain, especially the kind of pain he'd inflicted that night long ago. But most of all, he wanted her to know how special and desirable she was, and how blessed he would feel if she'd forgive him for hurting her and consider the possibility of them together. He broke the kiss, looked into her eyes and said, "Please, Mandy. Give me another chance."

She placed her hand on his cheek. "It isn't just because of Kaden?"

"No, but it's only better because of Kaden," he said honestly.

She glanced down, as though thinking about his words and their past and whether or not she believed everything he truly meant. Then blessedly, she looked back up at him and smiled. "Then, okay."

Chapter Twelve

The Cutter farm was ten miles from Claremont, about halfway to Stockville and surrounded by an evergreen forest. A split rail fence bordered the lengthy dirt road leading to the log cabin, and a pond even larger than the fishing hole held a formidable spot on the left side of the property. An abundance of white cows and one big black bull grazed in one of the fields, while donkeys and horses meandered around the edge of another, their baying and neighing filling the air as Mandy slowly drove toward the house. Large round hay bales dotted the entire span of the property as far as Mandy could see, and Lookout Mountain created a backdrop that made the whole scene photo-ready. She itched to have her camera in hand. The setting was a photographer's dream.

Parking near the house, she exited her car to find Casey Cutter standing on the front porch. He waved and grinned broadly, comfortable in his surroundings and blending perfectly in a dark green Western shirt, blue jeans, boots and cowboy hat. This look suited him much better than the baseball uniform he'd worn to her gallery, and she was glad that John suggested the farm for his senior photos.

"Hey, Miss Mandy," he said, one side of his mouth crooking up as he stepped from the porch and walked toward her car. "Can I help you carry something?"

"No, I have everything I need right here," she said, patting the camera bag. She took another glance around. "This place is amazing."

He grinned, shrugged broad shoulders. "We like it out here, even if it does take a lot of work."

"You do it all yourselves? You and John?" she asked, thinking the place looked too large and way too neat to be maintained by a teen in high school and his big brother. The log cabin was similar to the wilderness lodge she'd built with Kaden, the barn lined with stalls that appeared to house several horses, the fields covered well over a hundred acres and everything looked picture-perfect.

"John's not here a whole lot anymore," Casey said, and his smile slipped a tad with the statement. "He's working nearly all day every day with every job he can find." He looked away from Mandy, toward the mountains. "The farm holds its own, but John's got plans for me to go to college and has been trying to get the money together. That's why he's working so many extra jobs." He emitted a barely audible sigh. "I'd be content to stay here and work the farm like I do now, but John didn't get to go to college and says he doesn't want me to miss out."

Mandy was impressed on several levels. One, that John was giving everything he had to take care of his younger brother. And two, that a teen who was involved in school, baseball and church could also take care of a place this size.

This was what family—a real family—did for each other, and this was what she wanted to do for Kaden always. Provide for him and make sure that he had what he needed. Would she work three jobs if necessary to make that happen, like John was doing? It didn't take but a moment to have the answer. Sure she would. But then again, she wouldn't be raising Kaden alone. She had Daniel…

"So, you ready to take some pictures?" Casey asked. "I didn't really think I needed any, but John kind of makes his mind up about something and there's no arguing with him."

"Well, I think it's great that he's making sure your pictures are done," she said, trying to decide where they should begin. "There's so many great backgrounds to choose from, it's hard to know where to start."

"Well, if it's okay with you, I'd like to get Sam in at least one of them."

"Sam?"

"Come on, I'll introduce you." Casey started walking toward the barn with Mandy following close behind. They entered the wide entrance, and she inhaled a combination of hay, alfalfa and sweet feed. Her grandparents had given Mandy and Mia riding lessons when they were little to entertain them during the summer. Mandy couldn't remember the location of the farm where they'd taken lessons, but she remembered the smells. And she remembered how happy she'd been riding the horse named Pepper.

"I need to bring Kaden out here," she said,

wishing now that she'd have brought him along instead of leaving him with Daniel. She'd thought he'd be bored, but now she realized that he'd be anything but.

"You can bring him out any time you want," Casey said, grabbing some molasses treats from the feed room and dropping them in his shirt pocket. "I met him this morning at church. Cute kid."

"You met Kaden?"

"Yeah, he came to our classroom to see his uncle after he got done in his class, and Nadia introduced him to everyone. He was all excited about everything he learned and Mr. Brantley let him tell us about it." Casey grinned. "He really liked his class."

"Yes, he does." Mandy continued following Casey through the barn, but her mind drifted to this morning when Kaden and Daniel left for church. She'd thought they looked so nice all dressed up and ready to go, and she tried to make herself feel good about the fact that they were going together and were both so happy about it.

But she'd seen an expression on Daniel's face when they waved goodbye that could only be described as sad. He didn't have to say a word and Mandy still knew how badly he wanted her to go, as well. And now, hearing how excited Kaden had been after class and how he shared that excitement with Daniel's class, she kind of wished she'd have been there.

But not because she needed church or forgave God for letting everything go so wrong over the past few years. So going back to church right now wouldn't be right. She couldn't, no matter how badly Daniel wanted her to or how much she missed the two of them when they were gone.

"Miss Mandy, this is Sam. Sam, this is Miss Mandy," Casey said, pulling her attention back to the here and now. He'd made it to the other end of the barn, where a tall red horse had obviously seen him coming and galloped in from the field. The horse nudged Casey's head and then immediately sniffed Casey's shirt pocket. "You are one spoiled girl," Casey said, grinning as he fished a treat out of the pocket and gave it to the horse.

"Her name is Sam?" Mandy asked, already lifting her camera and snapping pictures of the horse with Casey. The sun slipped low in the distance and put the horse and master in an exquisite silhouette.

"Short for Samantha," Casey said. "My dad

bought her for Landon, and Landon was a little sad she wasn't a stallion. So she became Sam."

"Landon?"

"Our oldest brother. He's serving in Afghanistan," Casey said. "Been there since everything happened with Mom. Well, not always in Afghanistan, but in the Army, you know."

Of course. Mandy remembered Landon, but she'd practically forgotten about the oldest Cutter son. He had already joined the Army by the time she started high school, but she'd seen him around town growing up and, naturally, at church. Plus, now that Casey mentioned him, she also recalled a few trophies and plaques at the high school that bore his name. "He played football, right?"

"All County, All State," Casey said. "All pretty much everything," he added with a grin, while Sam received another treat.

For the next hour they worked their way around the farm, with the fields, mountains, animals and setting sun all providing stunning backdrops for Casey's senior portraits. Mandy suspected that the pictures she'd taken today would be some of her best yet.

"Okay, I think I've got plenty of good ones,"

she said, after they took a few final shots of Casey on the porch with John's old hound dog Lightning dozing near his boots.

"I'm sure that'll make John happy," Casey replied.

"John already gave me his contact information so we should be all set. Nadia will email the proofs when they're ready, and you can let me know which ones you decide on."

"Maybe I could come in and pick them out at your store," Casey said hopefully, undoubtedly wanting to find a way to spend a little more time with Nadia.

Mandy grinned. "That'd be even better."

"Nadia works there every day after school, right?" he asked.

"Yes, she does," Mandy said, noticing the way his amber eyes lit up when he said her name. Young love was so sweet. "You like Nadia, huh?"

"Yeah, I like her," he said, his voice dropping off a little toward the end as though he wanted to say more.

"But?" Mandy prompted, unable to stop herself from wanting to know why he was having such a hard time simply asking Nadia out on a date. He'd made a weak effort by asking the pretty girl if he could give her a ride home, but Nadia was sixteen and old enough to date. What was holding Casey back?

When he didn't readily answer, Mandy asked again, "But what, Casey?"

He gave her that one-shoulder shrug. "But she's really, well, good."

Mandy felt like she was looking in a mirror. Casey didn't think he was right for Nadia because she was a good girl. Mandy had often questioned whether she was right for Daniel, because he was so amazingly good. But she now believed she was exactly right for him, and she also believed Casey could be exactly right for Nadia. "And you aren't good?" she asked.

"I'm…trying," he said, one corner of his mouth lifting into a half smile.

Loud music and a roaring engine broke through the peaceful sounds of the farm and caused Mandy to forget whatever she'd been about to say next. Instead, she followed Casey's gaze toward the dirt road, which was becoming a long cloud of dust as a black sports car buzzed toward the house.

"Goodness," Mandy said, and she looked at Casey to see he'd tossed his cowboy hat on a nearby chair and untucked his shirt. He shook his head then slung his hair to one side, while the car jerked to a stop a few feet from Mandy's car and sent an even bigger dirt cloud up toward the porch.

Mandy squinted past the temporarily gritty air then blinked a couple of times while the smoke cleared.

"These are my friends," Casey said, his words low enough for only Mandy to hear. "I'm, uh, going out with them for a while. We're done here, right?"

His tone had changed. His smile had turned kind of cocky. And the sweet teen she'd seen merely minutes ago, photographed for an entire hour, essentially disappeared as he nodded a curt greeting to the other guys waving him toward the car.

"Hey, man, you coming or what?" the driver called.

Then another teen in the passenger seat grinned at Mandy. "Hey, you can come, too, if you want. Gonna be a good time." He raised his brows suggestively, and Mandy felt her skin grow cold.

"No, thank you," she said, then she turned away from the car and looked at Casey, who'd already started locking up the house and readying to leave. "You sure you want to go out with them?" she asked, whispering her words. But that probably didn't matter, since the kids in the car had already cranked the music back up to a fever pitch.

"They're my friends," Casey repeated. Then he sighed, looked at Mandy and added, "Thanks for coming out to take the pictures."

"You're welcome," she answered, watching him head toward the car and climb inside. She stood there on the porch while the carful of kids tore out of sight and she wondered what she'd do one day if Kaden, her beautiful little Kaden, had friends like those guys.

Trouble. That's what she'd seen when she saw those guys in the car. And when she'd seen Casey earlier, chatted with him throughout the photo shoot, she'd seen a good boy. A boy who worked hard and was respectful and deserved a good girl like Nadia. The problem was, when he climbed in that car and waved goodbye, the good boy had all but disappeared.

Chapter Thirteen

"Chad and Jessica asked if Kaden could go home with them tonight after T-ball practice and play with Nathan for a while." Daniel stood in Mandy's kitchen while they waited for Kaden to get his baseball bag from his room.

"Is that your way of asking for a date?" They hadn't had any alone time since Saturday, so Mandy was glad for Chad and Jessica's offer. She'd missed being in Daniel's arms, had yearned to be close to him again. And she'd replayed that kiss continually in her thoughts ever since they'd left the fishing hole.

"I suppose you can count it as a date," he said with a smile, "since we're starting with dinner." His throat pulsed as he swallowed thickly, and Mandy sensed a hint of nervousness in his tone.

An excited little ripple worked through her skin. What was he planning tonight? And did she dare hope that he was ready to make this relationship more serious? As in…more permanent, maybe? She couldn't control her grin. "So, what's after dinner, then?" She imagined him taking her to Hydrangea Park, telling her he couldn't stop thinking about the two of them together from now on, loving each other and loving Kaden. Her smile was practically uncontainable now.

"The thing is, I'm not sure how you'll feel about what I was thinking for tonight, but it'd mean a lot to me if you'd trust in me enough to give it a try."

Okay, that didn't seem like the way he'd ask her to a romantic night by the heart-shaped pond and gazebos at Hydrangea Park. "What would mean a lot to you?" she asked, then added, "Give what a try?"

"I'm ready to go!" Kaden yelled, running into the kitchen wearing every bit of his baseball gear, from the batting helmet on his head to the glove on his hand to the cleats on his feet.

Mandy laughed. "Kaden, the reason we got you that new equipment bag at Mr. Bowers's shop is so you can carry everything to the field easily. Was there anything left to put in the bag?"

The bag dangled limply at his side. "Yeah, my water bottle."

Daniel smiled. "He got you there, Mandy."

"So let's go!" Kaden stood by the door bouncing back and forth from one cleat to the other. "Come on! We can't be late!"

"No, that probably wouldn't be good, since I'm the coach," Daniel agreed with a laugh.

Mandy glanced down at her outfit, Daniel's old Rangers jersey and cutoff jeans. Not exactly what she planned to be wearing if Daniel were taking her out for a romantic dinner. But he'd said he wanted her to give something a try. What was it? "Should I change? Or bring different clothes for later?"

"Nah, you're fine. I'm wearing these," he said, indicating his coaching shirt and shorts.

"So what are we doing after dinner exactly?" she asked, her curiosity getting the best of her as they followed Kaden to the truck.

"I'll tell you later," he said, glancing toward Kaden, maneuvering his head to the side while attempting to get the helmet through the door.

Mandy really wanted to know what he'd

planned, but obviously Daniel didn't want Kaden privy to it. She didn't know whether to be excited or concerned about that fact.

T-ball practice lasted just over an hour, and Chad and Jessica were already waiting for them at the truck when they finished. "My practice was earlier," Nathan said to Kaden, "so we got to come over and watch you hitting some. Did you see us watching?"

"No, I was just listening to Uncle Daniel and watching the ball. That's what I'm supposed to do at practice."

"Wow, sounds like you've got your coaching game all set," Chad said to Daniel.

"He's still so excited about playing that he listens to every word I say," Daniel explained with a grin.

"Hey, I listen to what you say, too," Nathan said to his dad.

Chad squeezed his son's shoulder. "Yeah, you do." He looked at Kaden. "So you want to go with us for some pizza and then come over and play awhile with Nathan?"

"Sure do!" Kaden hugged Daniel and Mandy, and they waved as he piled into the SUV with Chad, Jessica, Nathan and Lainey.

Mandy waited until they'd left, then she turned toward Daniel, leaning against the side of his truck. "Okay," she said, "what have you got planned, or is it a surprise?"

"I'm thinking it'd be best if I didn't surprise you with this," he said.

Mandy didn't like the way that sounded. "With what?"

"Chad called me earlier today and reminded me about the support group that meets tonight at Stockville Community College. He asked if you and I wanted to give it a try, and he offered to take care of Kaden while we go."

Mandy hadn't realized how high her hopes had been until they plummeted. "You want me to go to a support group for people who've lost someone to drunk driving?" Her head involuntarily shook, even though she still hadn't voiced her refusal. Then she told him, "You know I can't go."

He audibly exhaled. "Why can't you, Mandy?" The concern in his voice touched her heart, but it didn't change her mind.

"Because that group's goal is to get me to move beyond Mia's death, to help me somehow forgive—forget—or whatever. I've read about support groups like that online. I've also gotten all of their pamphlets from whoever keeps mailing them my way. But I don't need a support group. I know I can't forget. I won't ever forget. And the drunk that hit Mia and Jacob died on the way to the hospital. It isn't like he's asked for my forgiveness."

"Mandy, he never had a chance to ask."

She continued to shake her head. "Daniel, how can you ask me to go to a group like that? Doesn't it still hurt you, the way it hurts me? How are we supposed to get with those other people and act like everything is okay? Everything isn't okay." She closed her eyes, frustrated that she was taking it out on him, when he'd been through the same thing. "I'm sorry, Daniel. I don't mean to make it sound like I don't appreciate what you're doing. I do. But I'm not ready for that. You and I are different that way. You forgive and forget easier. I don't. And I don't think I ever will."

"Mandy, will you hear me out on why I think this is important?" he asked, taking her hand. "Come on, let's sit and talk for a minute."

Her jittery heart seemed to calm down a bit when his hand closed around hers, the warmth of his fingers enveloping her own and making her feel more at ease. "Daniel, I know you mean well, but you're asking too much. Let's go have dinner tonight and spend some time together, like we did on Saturday. I loved that, and I really want to be with you, just not at that support group."

He guided her to the bench, sat down and tenderly took her other hand, as well. Those brilliant blue eyes captured hers and studied her for a moment before he finally spoke. "I had planned to talk to you about this tonight, at the end of the night," he said. "But I need you to know everything, how I'm feeling now and what I'm thinking about us and our future."

A tremor of hope touched her heart. He *was* thinking about a future with her. "Okay."

"Mandy, spending time with you over the past week, especially at the fishing hole on Saturday, has made me realize several things about myself and about how I feel about you." He smiled. "How I believe I've felt about you for quite some time, even if I wasn't willing to admit it."

Mandy held her breath, fearing what he might say while also hoping to hear the words she dreamed Daniel Brantley would one day profess to her.

"Mandy, I've been attracted to you for as long as I can remember," he said, a slight smile playing with his lips as he spoke. "I'm fairly certain I've also been fighting that attraction for as long as I can remember, because I didn't think you knew what you wanted back then. And I didn't know if you were what I needed, with your eagerness to see the world and to leave everything behind."

She opened her mouth, but he moved his finger to her lips and gave her another grin.

"Hear me out first, please," he repeated.

Mandy nodded, enjoyed the feel of that finger against her lips for another moment, then kept her mouth shut when he eased it away, sliding it along her jawline and down her throat.

"You're so beautiful," he whispered longingly. He paused a moment, then continued, "This past week I've realized that you don't have to leave Claremont to be happy, that what you've needed was to have a reason to stay. And Kaden—and hopefully now I— have given you that. I want to stay here, too, Mandy, with you. I want to raise Kaden with you, and I want us to be a part of each other's lives completely."

Mandy felt her heart pound in her chest. "I want that, too."

"But there's something missing, Mandy,

and I think you feel it, too." When she didn't say anything, he said, "I'm a man of God. He's called me to preach his word, and I plan to do that until the day I die. And I can't see myself in a lifelong relationship—a marriage—with anyone who doesn't trust in Him." His eyes misted over, and the sight pierced Mandy's heart.

"Mandy, I love you. I've realized that over the past few days, and I think I've loved you for quite some time. I was just fighting it. But I need God in any relationship that I'm in—I don't think a marriage can survive without Him. And I think you may blame Him for what happened with Mia."

"I blame the guy that got behind the wheel drunk," Mandy said quickly, her emotions in a tailspin. Daniel had finally told her that he loved her, something she'd dreamed about for most of her life. And then he'd told her it wouldn't work. The pain of that was worse than the knowledge that she finally had his love.

"But if you didn't blame God, too, why can't you pray? And why won't you go to church with me and Kaden?"

She couldn't answer, because she couldn't

deny the truth. She did blame God. She blamed God and she blamed that thoughtless guy that climbed behind the wheel that night and took Mandy's last link of family. And right now, she blamed God for causing her to be so warped that Daniel didn't think they could have a relationship.

"How do you think that going to that support group will help?" she asked, grasping at straws and already knowing she was coming up short. She couldn't go to that meeting. She just couldn't.

"You need to forgive, Mandy," Daniel said. "You need to forgive the guy that made a horrible mistake that cost Mia and Jacob their lives. And you need to stop blaming God and start letting Him help you through the pain. He's the only one that can make it better."

She shook her head. "And unless I can do that, you can't love me."

"Mandy, I don't think there's anything that could make me stop loving you now. But I can't have a relationship with you, not the kind I want to have, if you won't let God in. And to do that, you need to forgive."

She finally had everything she'd ever wanted. Kaden. Daniel. Daniel's love. But even the thought of having all of that didn't take away the pain of everything she'd lost. "I'm sorry, Daniel. I can't."

Chapter Fourteen

For two weeks, Mandy and Daniel took turns keeping Kaden depending on their work schedules or what Kaden had going on with T-ball and church. Every time they saw each other, it was simply to take care of Kaden's needs, and despite the circumstances, they did their best imitation of normalcy.

But Mandy suspected that Kaden was on to the change, because his prayers at night had now started including the same simple phrase.

Please bless Aunt Mandy and Uncle Daniel and help them be really really happy again.

And each and every time Daniel picked Kaden up for church, Daniel asked the same thing. "Come with us, Mandy. Please."

And she'd answered with the same exact words she'd said two weeks ago. "I can't."

Ditto for the trips to the support group meetings. Daniel would call and ask Mandy to come give it a try, tell her how much it was helping him heal. And Mandy would turn him down again. She couldn't forget, and she couldn't forgive. And because of that, she couldn't have the relationship she wanted with Daniel.

It hurt her heart, but that was how things were. The only blessing was that Daniel hadn't said anything else about pursuing custody of Kaden. Apparently since he now believed she wasn't leaving town and since she was willing to share Kaden's time, he was okay with that. Thank goodness. She couldn't handle fighting with Daniel over Kaden. She didn't want to go through that kind of pain, and she didn't want Kaden to go through it, either. More than that, she just didn't want to fight with Daniel.

She wanted to love him.

"Aunt Mandy, can dreams change?"

Mandy had been tying the laces on Kaden's cleats to get him ready for his first official game, but her hands paused and she looked up at his concerned face. This was his first day back with her after spending the weekend with Daniel, and now she wondered if he and

Daniel had had some discussion on dreams and Daniel had forgotten to clue her in. "Can they change?" she repeated blankly.

He nodded. "Yeah, like, if your dream changes a little is it still the same dream? Or is it a different dream, then?"

She had to think about that one. She let her hands continue the process of tying his shoes while she pondered the answer, then she finally said, "I think it's still the same dream."

"Okay."

After she'd double-knotted both shoes, she asked, "Kaden, are you talking about your dream?"

"Yeah. I think it's about to happen, but then I got to thinking that it isn't really the same dream anymore. So I didn't know if it still counted when it comes true. If it can change a little, then it almost happened one time already."

Mandy felt as if she was attempting to solve a puzzle with key pieces missing. "It almost happened?"

He nodded cryptically.

"When?" she asked.

"Saturday."

Okay, Saturday. They'd spent the morning at the T-ball field for a practice game and then he'd gone back home with Daniel since she had several photo shoots that afternoon. She couldn't recall anything at the T-ball field that would have potentially been Kaden's dream. So something must have happened that afternoon with Daniel, but Daniel hadn't mentioned anything.

Her mind whispered that if she and Daniel were together, really together, then she probably wouldn't have missed Kaden's big moment.

A knock at the back door signaled Daniel's arrival.

"Hey, he's here. It's almost time for the first game!" Kaden said, running to the door and flinging it open. Then he stepped back from Daniel and held his arms wide. "I'm ready! The real uniform and everything!"

"Yes, you certainly are," Daniel said, squatting down to eye level with Kaden. "Give me a hug. This is a big day."

Kaden jumped into his arms, while Mandy's heart pulled in her chest.

"You ready to go?" Daniel asked Mandy.

She blinked. Okay, she had thought since he and Kaden were going an hour early to make sure everything was ready for the game, she would simply drive over later.

But he was including her in the early arrival. Since that night when he'd confessed his love and then she'd refused to forgive, they hadn't been in a vehicle together. She'd missed the closeness of riding to the field and of simply feeling like a real family. Her throat tightened, and she swallowed past the burn of oncoming tears.

"Mandy?" Daniel asked again.

"Come on, Aunt Mandy. We gotta hurry!"

"Yes, I'm ready," she said. "Let me just go tell Nadia that I'm leaving." Thrilled to be included in Daniel and Kaden's trip to the field, Mandy darted up front to find her new employee.

Nadia looked up from the computer, grinned and said, "We just received John Cutter's order for Casey's pictures. He picked the same ones that I thought were best."

"That's great," Mandy said.

"Casey really takes great pictures, doesn't he? I mean, it looks just like him, but on the farm he looks so relaxed and at ease, especially when he's with his horse, don't you think?"

"Yes, I do," Mandy said, wanting to hurry back to Daniel and Kaden but not wanting to be rude to the sweet girl. Nadia had proven to be a godsend, always working, always smiling.

"Did I hear Mr. Brantley back there?" Nadia asked.

"Yes. It's Kaden's first ball game, and they've asked me to ride with them to the game. Can you lock up when you leave?"

"Sure," Nadia said, her smile widening. "I'm glad you're all going together." She'd sensed Mandy's sadness over the past two weeks and had undoubtedly put two and two together.

"Thanks, Nadia."

"My folks said that Casey can pick me up tonight, and we're going to a movie, I think," Nadia said brightly.

"I'm glad. Have a good time."

"I will."

Mandy grabbed her camera bag then hurriedly returned to the back of the store. Daniel and Kaden sat buckled up in the truck, Kaden once again wearing his batting helmet while traveling. She locked the back door, sprinted to the truck and jumped in the front seat.

"Everything okay?" Daniel asked, backing out of the parking space.

Mandy nodded. "Yes," she said. Everything was okay. Not exactly the way she wanted it to be, but much better than she'd anticipated.

She was riding to Kaden's first T-ball game with Daniel, and even if he couldn't give her the happily-ever-after she wanted, at least he could give her this.

In fifteen minutes, they were at the field. Daniel parked the truck, got out and watched as Kaden crawled across the seat and jumped to the ground. "You ready for your first game?" Daniel asked.

"Am I!" Kaden said, smiling from ear to ear. "I'm gonna hit it hard and run fast and not get out!"

Daniel held up a palm, and Kaden gave it a high five. "Sounds great."

Mandy was so grateful that Daniel brought her to the game early so she could witness every moment of this memory with Kaden. She waited for Kaden to move to the back of the truck and climb up on the tailgate to start tossing out bases, bats, and gloves. Then she stepped closer to Daniel and murmured, "Thanks."

He didn't ask why she was thanking him; he simply said, "There are going to be times when we should all be together. This is one of those times." Then he looked again at Mandy. "You're still adorable."

She had on his old baseball jersey, a pair

of blue jean shorts and a baseball cap with her ponytail poking through the back. She'd hardly put on any makeup, because it was getting pretty hot out, and she figured she'd probably sweat it all off at the field. "I think you're being nice," she said.

"I think I'm being honest." His words warmed her completely, even more when she noticed his eyes linger on her lips. "I've missed you, Mandy. And I don't know what to do about where we are."

"I've missed you, too," she said. Hadn't been able to eat. Hadn't been able to sleep. But also hadn't been able to bring herself to go to one of those meetings, step one foot in church or even pray. "And I don't know what to do about it, either." She knew what he wanted her to do, but she just didn't see how that would ever happen if she had no desire for any of that.

It didn't take long before the Rangers and the Marlins began gathering on the field. Kaden ran there, and Mandy helped Daniel get all of the equipment situated in the dugout before his team took their positions. "Kaden really wants to score today," she said.

"I'm betting he will," Daniel said. "That's the great thing about T-ball. The kids are still learning how to get each other out, and usually the innings end not because of three outs but because a team reaches the five-run limit."

"Well, he said his dream might come true today, so I'm thinking that might be it, to score in a real game," Mandy said.

"You might be right," Daniel mused. "You brought your camera, right?"

"Oh, I left my camera in the truck. Be right back."

"Okay," he said, smiling and seeming more at ease with her than he'd been during the past two weeks. Maybe things would get a little better now. Mandy sure hoped so. Even if she couldn't have what she wanted, at least she could have a good relationship with Daniel for Kaden's sake.

Mandy got the camera and returned to find the Rangers all on the field with Daniel hitting baseballs for fielding practice. Kaden, one of the tallest on the team, stood in center field and had his hands on his knees, down and ready, the way Daniel had taught him.

Then the Marlins began warming up. Both teams tossed the ball around the field and pretty much every player ran from his or her position to try to field the ball. It was hysterical and endearing.

Finally the first player came up to bat, and Mandy watched the little girl hit the ball to center field, straight to Kaden. His fellow players in left field, in right field and the girl playing second all turned and started running toward the ball while Daniel tried to get their attention and tell them to stay put. None of them were having any part of that; they all wanted the ball. But Kaden ran up and got to it first then threw it as hard as he could toward the other team's dugout. Mandy snapped several pictures of him fielding the ground ball.

Kaden saw her with the camera and waved wildly after he tossed the ball, which caused even more laughter in the stands. Since Kaden's throw put the ball in the opposite dugout, the batter consequently moved to second base before Kaden's first baseman was able to get the ball and run it all the way to the pitcher.

The stands roared with cheers and laughter, everyone enjoying the sweetness of seeing the kids learn the game.

Mandy snapped photo after photo of Kaden and his teammates throughout several innings. And in the third inning Kaden not only got on base but three teammates after him also got on, which put him crossing home plate amid the cheers of Mandy and the remainder of fans watching the game, which included Jessica, Nathan and Lainey, since Daniel had recruited Chad to be a base coach.

When Kaden got back to the dugout, Mandy zoomed in with her camera and got another great shot.

"Aunt Mandy, did you see me?" he called, his face pressed against the chain link of the dugout fence.

"Yes, Kaden, I did!"

"Did you see me, Nathan?"

"Yep, I saw you!" Nathan said. "Good job!"

"Wasn't it awesome?" Kaden yelled.

"It sure was!" Mandy yelled back, her heart bursting with pride.

Then the inning ended and they returned to the field, while Mandy tried to figure out exactly what composed Kaden's dream. In the fifth and final inning, she found out.

Kaden put on his batting helmet and took his practice swings while alternating between giving Mandy, Daniel and Nathan a thumbs-up after every rotation.

Daniel had recruited Mitch for a base coach,

and he stood to the right of first, while Chad stood to the left of third. The boy in front of Kaden made it to first, and then it was Kaden's turn to bat.

Kaden gave everyone another thumbs-up as he moved to the batter's box, and Daniel put the ball on the tee. Mandy listened as Daniel gave him the same instructions he'd been giving him every day at practice.

"Keep your eye on the ball," he said. "Hit it hard and then run as fast as you can to first. Then listen to Coach Mitch so he can tell you whether to keep going or stop. Okay?"

Kaden's heavy helmet bobbed. "Okay!"

"And have fun," Daniel added.

"I will!"

"Here we go, Kaden!" Nathan yelled. "Hit it hard!"

Mandy joined in. "Come on, Kaden! You can do it, honey!" She got up and moved down by an opening in the fence so she could get a clearer photo of him hitting the ball.

Kaden lifted the bat and swung, wasting no time at all connecting with the ball, which shot across the field in a hard line drive between first and second. Kaden ran so hard Mandy thought his huge helmet might cause him to topple forward, but he managed to stay upright and landed on first base.

"Keep going!" Mitch yelled, waving his arms wildly to let Kaden know he had the go-ahead for second. Meanwhile, the second baseman, center fielder and right fielder had all left their spots and headed for the ball, still rolling toward the fence.

"Come to me, Kaden!" Chad yelled from third. "And run fast!"

Mandy snapped picture after picture and tried to keep her hands steady while her whole body shook. The World Series couldn't be more exciting than this!

The little girl playing right field finally got to the ball, turned around and threw it as hard as she could...toward first base. The first baseman went running for the ball, while the catcher yelled, "Throw it here!" And while Chad also yelled, "Keep going, Kaden! Fast, fast, fast!"

Mandy saw Kaden's jaw clenched as he rounded third base and ran in a frenzy toward home plate. Daniel moved out of the dugout toward home and cheered him on. "Keep going, Kaden! Keep going!"

The boy playing first threw the ball to the right of home plate, and the catcher scurried to get it, but he didn't stand a chance against Kaden. Mandy's heart was in her throat as she watched her nephew running as hard as he could, stomping on home plate with both feet, then turning to Daniel's outstretched palms and giving him two high fives. Daniel lifted him up and swung him around, while the crowd cheered and Mandy rapidly snapped away.

"A home run!" she yelled, tears trickling down her cheeks at Kaden's amazing feat. "You did it, Kaden! A home run!"

Daniel finally put him on the ground, and Kaden ran to the dugout, where his teammates all cheered and applauded.

Mandy moved behind the dugout and kept taking pictures as Kaden accepted all of the hugs, slaps and congratulations from his team. Then he took off the batting helmet and looked at Mandy.

Smiling so big she was sure she saw every tooth, Kaden exclaimed, "I did it, Aunt Mandy!"

She wiped her cheeks. "You sure did!"

Then he grabbed his Gatorade from the bench, took a big sip and moved toward Mandy, who was still standing right behind the dugout. Tiny sweat droplets trickled from his temples as he looked at her through the chain-link fence and said, "Did you get it? Did you get my picture getting the home run?"

"I sure did," she said.

He took another sip, wiped his mouth with the back of his hand then smiled again. "That was my dream, Aunt Mandy. I can tell you now, because it came true."

"To get a home run?" she asked, while the stands got loud again for the little girl now batting.

He squished his nose, wiped his hand across his forehead and created a thick dirt smear in the process. "That was part of it."

"What was the other part?"

Sunlight filtering through the chain link caused him to squint as he looked at Mandy. "The other part was the hug at the end."

Daniel had been standing a few feet behind Kaden and was verbally coaching the little girl at home plate, but he turned and looked at Kaden. Mandy had no doubt he'd heard Kaden's words.

"I'm so glad your dream came true," she said, her voice thick with emotion.

"It was changed a little, but that's okay, right? You said that's still my dream, right?"

She nodded, but still wondered. "Kaden, how has it changed?"

"The hug at the end used to be with Daddy," Kaden exclaimed. "But now it's with Uncle Daniel. But that's okay, right? It's still my dream coming true, right?" he asked.

Mandy looked up to see Daniel's face tense, his mouth clenched as he looked at their sweet nephew. "Yes," she somehow managed to say. "It's definitely still your dream coming true."

Chapter Fifteen

The game ended not only with Kaden's dream coming true but also with the Rangers gaining their first victory, so Daniel called the group into the dugout and announced that he was treating them all to pizza. The cheers from the team were so loud that Mandy didn't hear her cell phone ring in her pocket, but she felt the phone's vibration, fished it out and answered.

"Hello?"

Someone said something on the other end, but Mandy couldn't hear over all of the noise.

"Hang on a minute," she said, covering her opposite ear and taking a few steps away from the cheering team to take the call. "Hello?"

"Mandy, is that you? Mandy Carter?"

"Yes, this is Mandy," she answered, recognizing the voice immediately. "Brother Henry?" She hadn't been in church in a while, but she remembered the kind man's tone from all those years of listening to him in the pulpit as a child.

"Mandy, I know Nadia's grown close to you over the past few weeks of working at your store, and I thought you'd want to know. She's been in an accident. A car wreck. She was with Casey Cutter, and he's okay, but Nadia is hurt. We're on our way to the hospital now…" He faltered for a moment but then continued, "We've put it on the prayer line at church, but I also wanted to give you a call in case, well, in case you want to come to the hospital. And Mandy, please pray for our sweet Nadia."

"How serious is it…?" She asked, struggling to keep her voice steady.

He paused, and Mandy heard the deep inhalation of someone crying, probably Mary, his wife. "They said she's unconscious. That's all we know."

"I'll be right there," Mandy said. "Thank you so much for calling."

Daniel had been talking to the team, but evidently he'd also been paying attention to Mandy, because he announced, "Let's see what Coach Chad and Coach Mitch want to say about your great game," and then he worked his way out of the dugout and to Mandy.

Mandy was so shaken she couldn't remember how she'd gotten to the game. Where was her car? She scanned the parking lot, but then recalled riding with Daniel. And she turned to find him right beside her, concern clearly visible on his face.

"What is it, Mandy? What happened? What can I do?"

"It's Nadia. She's been in an accident. She was riding with Casey and they had a wreck. I have to get to the hospital. She's hurt." Nadia's sweet smile, the look of how happy she'd been when Mandy had left earlier, swam through Mandy's thoughts. And right behind it, Brother Henry's words. "She's unconscious."

Mandy moved her hand to her mouth, because her cry was instant. "I don't even have my car here," she whimpered, "and I have to get there."

Daniel gathered her in his arms. "I'll get you there," he said. "I'm going, too." He yelled some instructions to Chad and Mitch while shuffling Mandy toward his truck, something about them taking the kids for pizza and Chad and Jessica taking Kaden home. He also told them to start praying for Nadia Berry, that she'd been in an accident and he'd keep them posted.

Daniel opened Mandy's door, and she climbed in the truck, then he darted to his side, jumped in and started the engine.

But something Brother Henry had said had pierced Mandy's heart, and she couldn't go another minute without doing what she believed Nadia needed most. "Wait," she said, reaching out to put her hand on Daniel's forearm.

He moved his foot to the brake and turned to Mandy. "What? What is it, Mandy?" He was so concerned, so ready to help in any way he could. And she was tremendously grateful, because she didn't know how she would do this alone; she needed Daniel's help and experience to guide her now.

"He asked me to pray for Nadia. Brother Henry asked me to pray. And I think I should. I think I need to, but I don't—I don't think I can do it myself." She had to do everything she could to help the sweet teen. "Will you please pray—with me—for Nadia?"

His eyes brimmed with emotion, and he

reached for her hands. "Yes, Mandy," he said, then bowing his head, he began, "Dear God, Heavenly Father, You know what's happened to Nadia, and You know how many people love her and care for her. You know how much Mandy and I love her and care for her. Please, Lord, be with Nadia now and with the doctors who are treating her. Guide them to do what they need to do to restore her from her injuries, Lord. Keep her safe, God, and help Mandy and I to say the right thing, do the right thing, for the family when we get to the hospital. In Your precious Son's name, amen."

He opened his eyes, and Mandy nodded. The touch of his hands had strengthened her, but his heartfelt prayer had given her hope. In her heart she did believe that God could help Nadia, and she did believe that He heard their prayer.

Daniel started the drive to the hospital, but Mandy closed her eyes tightly and continued praying.

God, I haven't talked to You much in the past few years, she started, as Daniel drove hastily to the hospital, *but please know that I mean these words. I want You to help Nadia, make her better, please, God.* She kept her eyes closed a few moments to think about Nadia and what a blessing she'd been in Mandy's life recently.

And God, please, help me. Help me to believe, and help me to be the person I need to be for Nadia. She opened her eyes, saw the intense look on Daniel's face as he drove. *And help me to be the person I need to be for Daniel. And Kaden. In Jesus's name, amen.*

They arrived at the hospital and hurried into the Emergency Room to find Brother Henry, his wife, Mary, and Nadia's parents. Mandy had met her parents several times when they came to pick Nadia up from work, and she'd really liked Brother Henry's son, Anthony, and his wife, Rachel, and admired them for their devotion to their family. Nadia was one of five children they'd adopted from various countries, and all of the kids had visited Mandy's gallery with them. She had never seen the couple without smiles on their faces…until now.

Mandy walked to them first. "I'm so sorry Nadia was hurt. Have you had any news? How is she now?"

Rachel's tears trickled steadily, and she emitted a low, "We just don't know."

Anthony draped a protective arm around

his wife. "They're doing some tests, but as of the last time the doctor came out here she still hadn't regained consciousness. She's pretty banged up, they said, but the important thing is for her to wake up, I think."

"We're praying," Brother Henry said.

"We're praying, too," Daniel said, and Mandy nodded, thankful that she had prayed. And she didn't plan to stop now.

God, please. Help her wake up.

Mandy looked up to see John Cutter coming out of one of the rooms in the rear of the emergency area. His face was taut and tense, and he shook his head as he neared. There was no doubt he was upset and had been crying.

"I'm—so sorry," he said, shaking his head as he spoke. "Anthony, Rachel. I—I'm so sorry. I'm praying for her. I'm not going to stop. Casey—he wants to talk to all of you. He asked if you'd go back and see him now, pray with him now for Nadia, if you would." John swallowed thickly. "But he said he'd understand if you don't want to see him now."

"No, of course we want to see him," Rachel said. "He's okay? We can go back now?"

"He's in room six," John said, his lower lip

rolling in with the words. "He—he needs to tell you something."

"All right," Brother Henry said. "Let's go, then."

The four of them moved down the hallway while John released pent-up tears, dropped into a nearby waiting room chair and put his head in his hands. "God, help her," he said aloud, while Daniel and Mandy both moved to him and squatted down in front of the chair.

"John, we're here for you, too," Daniel said, putting an arm around his friend.

John looked up, amber eyes still swimming in tears. "He's torn up, Daniel. And he should be. He went out with those guys, that rough crew, before he went to pick Nadia up, and he'd been drinking. That's what caused the accident. He'd been drinking and then he was driving too fast and lost control. They slammed into a tree on Nadia's side. I haven't seen her, but Casey said…" John shook his head again and looked heavenward. "Oh, God, Casey said he thought she was dead." A haunting gasp escaped John and he cried out, "God, please, help her."

Mandy's world tilted. Casey had been drinking. And he thought Nadia was dead.

No. This could *not* be happening again. She wanted to scream. She wanted to run. But most of all, she wanted God's help. She wanted—needed—to pray more. And Daniel must have known that John needed that, too, because he said, "Let's pray. All of us pray together right now, for God to heal Nadia and help Casey."

Mandy blinked at the last part. Help Casey? Casey had been drinking and that's what caused all of this. But she didn't voice her thoughts in front of John, and when they bowed their heads, she bowed hers, as well.

"Dear God," Daniel began, "You know Casey's heart. He made a mistake today, God. A horrible, terrible mistake. But he needs You now, Lord. You know he needs You now more than ever. Be with Him God, and hear his prayers for Nadia. Hear all of our prayers for Nadia, and heal her Lord. We know there is nothing You cannot do, so please, God. Heal Nadia. And Lord, please heal Casey's heart, too. In Jesus's name, amen."

Brother Henry, Mary, Anthony and Rachel returned to the waiting area and went straight to John.

"I'm so sorry," John said. "I've tried to talk to him, to teach him what he should and shouldn't do, but I'm afraid I haven't done a very good job."

Brother Henry shook his head. "John, that boy is in a lot of pain now. He feels responsible, and he knows he messed up. It isn't your fault, and Casey knows what he did and feels bad enough without us making it worse."

"Dad's right," Anthony said. "Casey is hurting, too." Tears fell down the man's cheeks, but he wiped them away. "He made a mistake, and he's praying his heart out for Nadia. That's what we're going to do, turn it over to God and pray for Him to give her back to us, safe and sound."

Rachel nodded. "We prayed with Casey."

Mandy was completely shocked at their words, but even more when Brother Henry looked to her and said, "We told Casey that you and Daniel were here, and he wants to see you both."

"Come on," Daniel said, taking Mandy's hand and leading her toward the curtain-covered rooms.

Mandy wasn't certain she was ready for this. She wanted to lash out at Casey and ask him what in the world he was thinking drinking and driving. She wanted to ask him if he understood that Nadia might be dying at this very moment—the way Mia and Jacob died last year—so she steadied her raging emotions and made her feet move alongside Daniel toward Casey's room.

Daniel slid the curtain aside, and Mandy saw the boy she'd photographed two weeks ago. But he didn't look like that same sweet, good-looking, carefree boy now.

He looked broken.

One eye was swollen shut, and the other was dripping tears and bloodshot. He had a thick white bandage circling his head and a sling holding his left arm. Two butterfly bandages centered his chin, apparently holding a broad gash in place.

But that wasn't what made him look broken. The sadness radiating from him, the anguish on his face, emanated intense pain.

"I messed up, Mr. Brantley," Casey choked out. "I don't know why. I don't know what I was thinking. I thought I was okay. I had only had a couple of beers, and I thought I was okay. And I didn't need them. Didn't even want them. And sure shouldn't have had them before picking Nadia up." His free fist slammed into the mattress and he let out an intense wail. "I really care about her. I've been wanting to go out with her for so long.

Tried to prove I could be good enough for her, but I'm not. And I never will be.

"I—I might have—I mean, oh man, have you heard how she is? She—she looked…" Another cry escaped, and his head tossed aside on the pillow. "I want y'all to pray for her. Please, please, pray. I'm asking God to save her. I don't want to live if she doesn't. I don't. I can't. I did it. I did that to her because I was so stupid."

Daniel moved to the bed. Mandy edged closer, too, and she found that her heart ached for the boy. He was falling apart, and he knew what he'd done was wrong. And when Daniel said, "We'll pray for her, Casey, but we're praying for you, too," Mandy nodded, her tears pushing free.

"Yes," she said, "we will."

They prayed with Casey, and then John returned to sit with him and they went back to the waiting room to continue praying and waiting with Nadia's family.

After a half hour, the doctor came out and told them all that Nadia hadn't regained consciousness and that he'd be back in another hour with an update, as well as with results from the tests they'd been performing since she was brought in.

"I'm going to the hospital chapel," Brother Henry said. Anthony, Rachel and Mary went, as well.

"We'll stay here and come get you all if the doctor comes out before the hour," Daniel assured them and was thanked by the family.

After they left, Daniel turned to Mandy and held out his arm, then waited for her to step into his embrace. The strength emanating from him, the exquisitely tender way he gathered her close, melted Mandy's heart.

"You okay?" he asked.

She nodded against his chest. "So worried about her," she managed. "She's so amazing, such a sweet girl." Mandy sniffed, then tilted her head to look at his face. "Daniel, I was so angry when John said Casey had been drinking. I kept thinking of that night, when I came here to be with Mia for the last time."

He nodded, kissed her forehead. "I know, honey. I thought immediately of Mia and Jacob, too."

"And when we walked back there to see Casey, I thought I wouldn't want to help him. I thought I'd be angry with him," she said, while Daniel nodded, giving her the time to express her feelings and holding her while she dealt with the emotions ravaging her soul.

"But then I saw him, and he's so hurt and so sorry for what he did. He knows that he made a mistake, and he's terrified that she isn't going to get better. And I got to know him over the past couple of weeks. He really is a good kid. It's just—" she swallowed "—he just made a terrible mistake."

Daniel nodded again. "Yes, he did."

"And after I saw him, and saw John's pain, too, then I remembered something else about that night last year."

"What did you remember?"

"I remembered when that other guy's parents showed up in the Emergency Room, and when the doctors came out and talked to them. I remember I was with Mia, but I heard that mother's scream for her son."

Mandy shook her head. "I didn't feel sorry for her. And I didn't feel sorry for him losing his life. He was only twenty-four, the same age as me, and he lost his life because he made a stupid mistake. And Mia and Jacob lost their lives because of his mistake. But it was a mistake. And I should have felt sorry for that family losing their son. I should have realized that he needed to be forgiven for his mistake, too." She inhaled, let it out. "Like Casey does."

Daniel drew her even closer, held her even tighter. "Oh, Mandy, I wish I'd have been with you last year when you went through all of that after the wreck. I hate it that you were alone and that I wasn't here when you needed someone so much."

"I haven't dealt with it well," she admitted, wiping more tears from her cheeks. "Have still been angry. Still blamed God for taking everyone I loved."

"And now you don't?" he asked.

"I don't blame Him for what happened, and I'm going to try to understand that the other guy made a fatal mistake," she said, then looked up again at Daniel. "That support group. Do they help you cope with it all? Deal with the pain and forgive?"

"Yes, they do."

"I want to go next time," she said, "if you wouldn't mind taking me."

"I wouldn't mind at all," he murmured, and softly kissed her hair.

"And Daniel," she added.

"Yes?"

"I thought I'd lost everyone I loved, but that isn't true. I still have Kaden." Her eyes studied him, and she touched a finger to his mouth, then whispered, "And I thank God that I have you. I love you, Daniel. I've loved you for a very long time."

"Oh, Mandy, I love you, too," he said, as a nurse entered the waiting room and asked, "Is Nadia Berry's family here?"

Daniel and Mandy turned toward the woman. "They went to the chapel," Daniel told her. "But we can go get them."

"Yes, please," the woman said, smiling broadly. "The doctor is still in with her, but he says they can come back now. She's awake and wants to see them."

"Praise God," Daniel said, grabbing Mandy's hand and hurrying down the hall toward the tiny chapel.

And Mandy grinned, repeated, "Praise God," and was thrilled to know that she'd never meant the words more.

Chapter Sixteen

Kaden's brows were raised so high they nearly disappeared beneath his sandy waves, and his smile was as wide as Mandy had ever seen, cheek to cheek. "Okay, I think that's almost our part now. Are you ready?" His excitement was palpable, as was his happiness. "Come on!" he urged. "We can't be late!"

Mandy laughed. "I love you, you know."

"Yep, I know, Aunt Mandy. And I love you, too. But we *cannot* be late!" He held his hand toward hers, and she clasped it.

"Ready," she said.

Kaden pulled at her arm and practically ran the entire way from Daniel's office to the church lobby. "See, the doors are open, so it's our time. That's what Brother Henry said."

"Yep, you're right," Mandy said. "It's our time."

They stepped between the open doors to the auditorium and Kaden gasped.

"Whoa, look at all those people!" he exclaimed, which caused a low rumble of laughter to trickle through the crowd.

"Yes, look at them all," Mandy said. Then she beamed at Brother Henry and Daniel, waiting at the front of the church.

"Ready to go?" Kaden asked, tugging at her hand once more.

"Definitely ready," Mandy replied, and she began the walk down the aisle, her hand clasping the little boy who'd become a huge part of her world, and her heart yearning for the man at the end of the aisle, the one who was patient enough to wait for her to find her way back home, to realize that Claremont was where she wanted to stay forever and to know that her life was nothing without love, and without God.

She passed lots of happy faces from the people around town, but the two smiles that touched her heart the most were from Casey and Nadia, standing beside each other and beaming at Mandy. It'd only been a month since the accident, but both teens were healing quickly. Casey had turned away from the rough crowd and turned to God, praising Him daily for Nadia's willingness to forgive.

Finally they reached the end of the aisle, and Kaden took Daniel's hand and then brought it to Mandy's the way he'd rehearsed last night.

"Now," Kaden said, "you're together."

Daniel grinned, looked at Mandy. "Yes," he murmured. "We are."

Mandy couldn't imagine life being any better than this, sharing it with the man she'd always loved and raising a little boy that they both adored. She smiled at Daniel, who didn't wait for Brother Henry's instruction to kiss the bride. He kissed her before Brother Henry even started talking, which caused another ripple of laughter in the crowd.

Then the ceremony began, and Mandy focused on remembering every word, every feeling, every tug at her heart. Because she was marrying the man she'd proposed to seven years ago. Back then she didn't truly understand the meaning of love. Now she did. And back then everything about that impromptu proposal had been wrong. But now, with Daniel, Kaden and, most importantly, God at the center of her world, everything couldn't be more picture-perfect.

Epilogue

"Look, Aunt Mandy, that's you!" Kaden exclaimed, running into the gallery and pointing to the gold easel that displayed the featured photographer.

Mandy wasn't certain whether she was more excited about being the featured photographer or about seeing her name beneath her picture.

Mandy Brantley. She'd been Mandy Brantley for six months now, but time didn't lessen the excited sensation she experienced every time she saw her new name.

"Adorable," Daniel whispered in her ear, then he said to Kaden, "Come on, let's go look at her pictures in the gallery."

"Aunt Mandy is a star, huh?" Kaden asked.

Mandy was already shaking her head in denial, but Daniel didn't miss a beat.

"Always," he said. "A star and a princess, too." He winked at Mandy. "Our princess."

They made their way through the outer lobby to the main exhibit area, where several people were already gathered around Mandy's group of photos.

"Isn't that lovely," one woman said.

"The theme is what really makes this work so well, don't you think?" a man returned.

Daniel took Mandy's hand, squeezed it, then leaned close to kiss her cheek. "It is a pretty amazing theme," he whispered.

They stopped walking, waited for the people to move away from the display and then finally got a chance to see her gallery exhibit.

There were several small photos that surrounded the center three, but those middle ones were the main key to the theme. They were what tied it all together. Mandy had printed all of them in black and white, because it added more depth, more passion to the already emotional scenes.

The first photo was of Kaden, swinging in Daniel's arms after his first home run. And the title beneath the photo…

Kaden's Dream.

* * *

The second photo was of Daniel, Mandy and Kaden in Malawi surrounded by children from the village churches, their smiles beaming amid their meager surroundings. The picture was taken three months ago on their first trip as a family to visit and help the churches Daniel started in Africa. And the title for that photo…

Mandy's Dream.

And the third photo was of Daniel, sitting at his desk at the church working on a lesson, while the window behind him displayed Kaden laughing and running on the playground outside. And the title…

Daniel's Dream.

The theme for the series hung above the three photographs, and the truth of the statement still caused her heart to clench.

Sometimes, dreams change.

She looked at Daniel and Kaden, her family, thought about the love that she'd been blessed with over the past year, and the peace that came with learning to forgive. Daniel had been patient with her, and God had, too, blessing her with Daniel's love and with a beautiful little boy. She touched her hand to her stomach and said another thank You to God, for He'd blessed her even more than she'd ever dreamed. A precious new life was growing inside of her, and she and Daniel couldn't wait to find out whether Kaden would have a little brother named Jacob or a little sister named Mia.

Either way, the new blessing to their family would undeniably be yet another dream come true.

* * * * *

Dear Reader,

When Jacob and Mia died, Mandy Carter's world was upended, her dreams were thrown out the window and she had to put another person's needs—her nephew, Kaden's— above her own.

This is the kind of challenge that everyone wants to believe they could handle. That this-is-what-my-life-is-now moment, where a person sees that they've been tossed onto a different path than they anticipated, and they accept that test and excel. Mandy grew emotionally and spiritually because of the hardship, and she became Kaden's princess, the one who took care of him when his mother couldn't, much like Pharaoh's daughter took care of Moses.

I enjoy mixing facts and fiction in my novels, and you'll learn about some of the truths hidden within the story on my website, www.reneeandrews.com. You can enter a contest on my site to win a painting by Gina Brown, the artist mentioned in the book and the person to whom this book is dedicated.

Additionally, my site includes alternate beginnings for some of my novels and deleted scenes that didn't make the final cut.

If you have prayer requests, there's a place to let me know on my site. I will lift your request up to the Lord in prayer. I love to hear from readers, so please write to me at renee@reneeandrews.com.

Blessings in Christ,
Renee Andrews

Questions for Discussion

1. In this book, Mandy's faith is tested when she loses her sister, Mia. Have you lost someone who was taken before their time? Did you turn to God? Or did you find yourself blaming God? What got you through the hardship of losing someone you loved?

2. Daniel feels called to share the Gospel abroad, but also to return to Claremont and help raise his nephew. Have you ever wondered if you were making the right decision regarding God's plan for you? How can you know whether the decision you make is best?

3. Mandy turned her back on God and then returned to Him. Have you ever gone away from God and then returned?

4. Teens are extremely influenced, both positively and negatively, by their peers and by the adults in their world. How was Casey influenced by his friends? Did his family situation play a factor in his will-

ingness to go along with the crowd? How did Daniel and Mandy influence Casey?

5. Why do you think Mandy found the willingness to forgive Casey when she hadn't been able to forgive the man who hit Jacob and Mia? How do you think she felt when she not only forgave Casey, but also the man who'd taken her sister's life?

6. Daniel managed to find a way to serve his ministry in Africa and also stay in Claremont and raise Kaden. Do you believe that God's plan sometimes involves creative thinking? How do you know that you're still following His plan and not just finding a way to do it your way?

7. The town of Claremont is composed of a small, tight-knit community where everyone knows everyone and cares for each other. How do you feel about life in a small town? Do you think it could benefit you spiritually?

8. The theme verse for this book is from Jeremiah: "For I know the plans I have for you, declares the Lord, plans to prosper you and not to harm you, plans to give

you hope and a future." What plan did God have for Daniel? For Mandy? What plan do you believe He has for you?

9. Mandy dealt with abandonment issues throughout her life. Have you ever had to come to terms with someone you cared about turning their back on you when you needed them? Or has someone you cared about died, and you felt that God— or even the person who passed away— somehow let you down?

10. The photos in Mandy's exhibit all depicted dreams that were changed. Have you ever had a dream or goal that began as one thing but ended as something totally different? What was that dream or goal? How did your dream change? Did it change for the better? And did that change benefit you physically, emotionally and/or spiritually?

LARGER-PRINT BOOKS!

**GET 2 FREE
LARGER-PRINT NOVELS
PLUS 2 FREE
MYSTERY GIFTS**

Love Inspired

Larger-print novels are now available...

YES! Please send me 2 FREE LARGER-PRINT Love Inspired® novels and my 2 FREE mystery gifts (gifts are worth about $10). After receiving them, if I don't wish to receive any more books, I can return the shipping statement marked "cancel". If I don't cancel, I will receive 6 brand-new novels every month and be billed just $4.99 per book in the U.S. or $5.49 per book in Canada. That's a saving of at least 23% off the cover price. It's quite a bargain! Shipping and handling is just 50¢ per book in the U.S. and 75¢ per book in Canada.* I understand that accepting the 2 free books and gifts places me under no obligation to buy anything. I can always return a shipment and cancel at any time. Even if I never buy another book, the two free books and gifts are mine to keep forever.

122/322 IDN FEG3

Name	(PLEASE PRINT)

Address	Apt. #

City	State/Prov.	Zip/Postal Code

Signature (if under 18, a parent or guardian must sign)

Mail to the **Reader Service:**
IN U.S.A.: P.O. Box 1867, Buffalo, NY 14240-1867
IN CANADA: P.O. Box 609, Fort Erie, Ontario L2A 5X3

Not valid to current subscribers to Love Inspired Larger-Print books.

**Are you a current subscriber to Love Inspired books
and want to receive the larger-print edition?
Call 1-800-873-8635 or visit www.ReaderService.com.**

* Terms and prices subject to change without notice. Prices do not include applicable taxes. Sales tax applicable in N.Y. Canadian residents will be charged applicable taxes. Offer not valid in Quebec. This offer is limited to one order per household. All orders subject to credit approval. Credit or debit balances in a customer's account(s) may be offset by any other outstanding balance owed by or to the customer. Please allow 4 to 6 weeks for delivery. Offer available while quantities last.

Your Privacy—The Reader Service is committed to protecting your privacy. Our Privacy Policy is available online at www.ReaderService.com or upon request from the Reader Service.

We make a portion of our mailing list available to reputable third parties that offer products we believe may interest you. If you prefer that we not exchange your name with third parties, or if you wish to clarify or modify your communication preferences, please visit us at www.ReaderService.com/consumerschoice or write to us at Reader Service Preference Service, P.O. Box 9062, Buffalo, NY 14269. Include your complete name and address.

LILP11B

Love Inspired.
SUSPENSE
RIVETING INSPIRATIONAL ROMANCE

Watch for our series of edge-
of-your-seat suspense novels.
These contemporary tales
of intrigue and romance
feature Christian characters
facing challenges to their faith...
and their lives!

AVAILABLE IN REGULAR
& LARGER-PRINT FORMATS

For exciting stories that reflect traditional values,
visit:
www.ReaderService.com

LISUSDIR11B